Rebecca's Heart

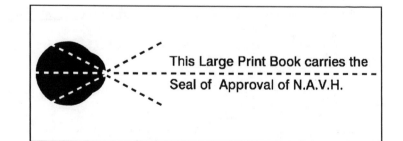

This Large Print Book carries the
Seal of Approval of N.A.V.H.

MASSACHUSETTS BRIDES, BOOK 2

REBECCA'S HEART

AN OLD-FASHIONED ROMANCE BLOOMS IN THE HEART OF NEW ENGLAND

LISA HARRIS

THORNDIKE PRESS
A part of Gale, Cengage Learning

GALE
CENGAGE Learning

Detroit • New York • San Francisco • New Haven, Conn • Waterville, Maine • London

GALE
CENGAGE Learning

LIBRARY OF CONGRESS CATALOGING-IN-PUBLICATION DATA

Harris, Lisa, 1969–
    Rebecca's heart : an old-fashioned romance blooms in the heart of New England / by Lisa Harris.
        p. cm. — (Massachusetts brides ; bk. 2) (Thorndike Press large print Christian fiction)
        ISBN-13: 978-1-4104-2758-8 (large print : hardcover)
        ISBN-10: 1-4104-2758-7 (large print : hardcover)
        1. New England—Fiction. 2. Large type books. I. Title.
PS3608.A78315R425 2010
813'.6—dc22   2010010611

Published in 2010 by arrangement with Barbour Publishing, Inc.

Printed in Mexico
1 2 3 4 5 6 7 14 13 12 11 10

To Mariah Lauren, my precious daughter. May you always seek Him first in everything you do. And to my fantastic critique partners. Thank you for taking this journey with me.

Prologue

Cranton, Massachusetts, 1883

"Rebecca Ann Johnson, I'm about to make you the happiest girl in the world." Jake Markham pulled an envelope out of his pocket and handed it to her.

"I thought I already was the happiest girl in the world." Rebecca clutched the envelope between her fingers and laughed. "I'm marrying you tomorrow, aren't I?"

Jake leaned across the blue cushioned sofa and stole a kiss. Her heart fluttered at the intimate gesture as she studied his familiar profile. Curly fair hair framed his smooth face. Square jaw, clear blue eyes. A solid, muscular form from helping his father work the Markham farm.

Mrs. Jake Markham.

Tomorrow she'd become his wife and someday, she prayed, the mother of his children. Heat rose to her cheeks, and she turned back to the gift.

"What is it?" Rebecca didn't try to hold back her enthusiasm as she drew two slips of paper out of the offered envelope. "Train tickets?"

"They're your wedding present. I planned to give them to you tomorrow after the ceremony, but I couldn't wait."

"I don't understand." Rebecca's brows scrunched together. She scanned the details on the train tickets, her excitement over the gift quickly waning. "These are one-way tickets to Portland, Oregon."

"Exactly. It's what we've always dreamed about, Rebecca." Jake leaned forward and grasped her hands. "There's plenty of land. We can settle somewhere along the coast if you'd like, or maybe in the Willamette Valley. It's supposed to be beautiful. Snow-capped mountains, forests of thick evergreen trees —"

"Wait a minute." Her mind spun with the implications of the tickets she held. "I know we've talked about the possibility of settling out west someday, but I never thought you were considering leaving now. These tickets are for next month."

"I know." Jake's face erupted with a smile. "My father gave us three hundred dollars for a wedding gift. We don't have to wait any longer."

Rebecca stood and walked to the large front window of her parents' gray-shingled farmhouse and took a steadying breath. Cranton, nestled in the lush Connecticut Valley of western Massachusetts, had been her home for all of her nineteen years. One day she dreamed of seeing more of the world, but right now she wanted to enjoy being married before she had to take on the responsibilities of settling somewhere else.

He didn't even ask me what I thought.

Her fingers touched the windowpane as she stared out across the lush acres of farmland bordered with stone fences. Tall elm trees and stately pines rose from the rich soil. Mayflowers dotted the apple orchards to the south. The white blossoms of the hydrangea bushes were beginning to fade but for now still held their beauty. This was her home. Jake crossed the room and stood beside her. "What's the matter, Rebecca? I thought you'd be excited."

Tears welled in her eyes. "You actually believed I'd be thrilled, despite the fact you never asked me what I thought before buying the tickets? I don't know if I'm ready to leave my family yet —"

"You're just nervous about tomorrow and not thinking clearly." Jake took another step toward her and ran his hand down the sleeve of her lavender day dress, but Rebecca pulled away. "We've talked about moving west —"

"You talked about it, and while I'm not against the idea, it was always something for us to consider for the future. Not now."

Unexpected anger seared through her like a hot iron. Her resentment didn't come from the fact he wanted to move away. She was hurt because he'd never asked her what she thought about leaving so soon after they were married.

Her hands curled into fists at her sides. "What in the world were you thinking, Jake Markham? Buying these tickets without even discussing the matter with me?"

"I thought you'd be happy."

The confused look that crossed his face didn't quell her anger. "What about my family and your father?" Rebecca paced across the hardwood floor to the other side of the room, pausing at the large stone fireplace. "Did you even stop to consider what they might think about this sudden move?"

"I've discussed it with my father, and he's excited for us. Told me if he were twenty years younger, he'd consider coming along." Jake raked his fingers through his hair. "If my mother were still alive, I know she'd feel the same way. As for your parents, I'm sure they'll be delighted you're getting such an opportunity."

"You've already told your father?" Folding her arms across her chest, Rebecca stomped her foot. "Is this how you see our marriage? You make all the decisions without even asking me what I think? Jake, I don't know if I can —"

He bridged the gap between them, and Rebecca felt his arms wrap around her. His lips pressed firmly against hers. For a moment she forgot why she was so angry as she yielded to his kiss. She loved Jake Markham and planned to spend the rest of her life with him. He was the one she'd dreamed of growing old with.

But he never considered asking me what I thought about the entire matter, Lord!

Rebecca pulled away from him, still feeling the pressure of his lips against hers. She touched her fingers to her mouth, the sweetness of his kiss slowly replaced by a swell of uneasiness in her heart.

"I thought this was what you wanted, Rebecca." His eyes pleaded with her to understand. "I just want to make you happy."

"No, Jake." She looked up at him and shook her head. "This is what you want. You don't know me at all."

And I don't know you either.

An hour later Rebecca smoothed her fingers across the silky white fabric of her wedding dress. She'd promised Jake she'd consider his decision, but today's experience had showed her something she now realized had been a part of their relationship all along.

She wanted a marriage like her parents'. Things hadn't always been easy for her father and stepmother. Both had lost their spouses years ago, and when they married each other, they brought seven children into the union. Still, despite the difficulties they'd faced, with God as the center of their relationship, they'd worked things out together.

That was the kind of marriage Rebecca wanted. Looking back, she realized this wasn't the first time Jake had made a decision concerning them both without consulting her first. Usually they were small incidences, but even when it came to the details of their wedding, Jake had made a number of decisions without her input.

He had been the one to set their wedding date and decide the minister from Springfield should perform the ceremony, not their well-loved preacher from Cranton. At the time it hadn't seemed to matter, but he always told her, never asked. It wasn't that she didn't respect God's roles for a husband and a wife, but could she live the rest of her life with a man who didn't respect her feelings?

Rebecca threw the dress on her bed and sat in front of her mirrored dresser. Undoing the French knot twisted at the back of her head, she began to brush out her long, dark hair. She'd allowed herself to get so caught up in the notion of being in love and taking care of wedding plans that she hadn't even noticed Jake's lack of concern over how she felt about matters. This time, though, he'd gone too far.

Suddenly everything was clear. If she married Jake Markham, she knew she'd be making the biggest mistake of her life. Her stomach clenched at the reality of what her decision meant. Come tomorrow, Jake would expect to see his bride walking down the aisle. Instead Rebecca planned on being as far away from that altar as the train could take her.

ONE

Eight months later

Rebecca held up the tailored slipcover for a closer inspection. Why couldn't her own life look as neat and orderly as the tiny, meticulous stitches in which she prided herself? She felt more like one of the jumbled spools of thread in her younger sister Sarah's sewing box. Twisted and tangled. Out of control.

She ran her fingers across the downy texture of the linen-and-cotton-blend fabric, fighting the all-too-familiar sense of restlessness. The indigo-on-white pattern of the lily blossom would work perfectly with Scarlet Bridge's padded chairs and sofa. *That* wasn't the source of her frustration. Already the material was beginning to take the shape of a stylish slipcover — one of Boston's fashion rages.

Rebecca finished the last few stitches of the chair cover and whispered a prayer of thankfulness that the front showroom of Macintosh Furniture and Upholstery was finally without customers. Despite their location on the outskirts of Boston, the store brought in a considerable number of wealthy clients from the city.

Letting out a deep sigh, she leaned back in her wooden chair and glanced around the showroom. Fine-quality chests of drawers made from imported wood, mahogany highboys, and dainty tea tables filled the room, along with a large assortment of bedsteads and dining tables. While many of the products the store sold were ready-made furniture, some, like the walnut dresser with its glossy marble top, were custom-made in the workroom in back of the store by Philip Macintosh and his four employees.

It wasn't as though she didn't enjoy working for her stepmother's best friend, Caroline Macintosh. Quite the contrary. She'd always found pleasure in taking a plain strip of fabric and turning it into something useful. Before she left home she'd been the one to sew the red gingham curtains that framed the large living room windows and the colorful slipcover that hid the faded sofa beneath it. Her father had always told her she had a knack for decorating, and she was thrilled she could finally put her talents to good use.

But for some reason even the enjoyment of working with Caroline to fill the numerous orders for slipcovers wasn't enough to squelch the edginess she felt inside.

Eight months ago she never would have imagined that she'd be sitting in Boston, surrounded by yards of brightly printed cottons and linens. At the time the invitation from Philip and Caroline had seemed like the perfect solution. Once everyone had recovered from the shock of her calling off the wedding, Jake used his train ticket and left for Portland. Four weeks later she arrived in Boston.

Clipping a loose thread with a pair of scissors, Rebecca shook her head. Shouldn't she at least have a twinge of guilt over breaking Jake's heart? She still felt certain that marrying him would not have been God's will for her life, but she had yet to discover His plan for her. Marriage and children had always been her dream, and she thought she'd found what she was looking for with Jake. That is, until he presented her with those train tickets without one thought as to how she might feel. How could she have been so wrong about someone?

The back door to the workroom opened,

pulling Rebecca out of her somber deliberations. Caroline, with her swollen abdomen and ever-pleasant smile, bustled into the room.

"Morning, Rebecca."

Rebecca set down the slipcover and forced a smile. "You're sure in high spirits today."

"I should be happy." Caroline hurried past a row of mahogany side chairs then stopped to catch her breath at the tailor's bench where Rebecca worked. "I'm married to the most wonderful man in the world, I'm going to be a mother in five weeks, and" — she dropped a copy of the *Boston Herald* on the table — "look at this."

"What is it?"

Caroline sank into a padded chair across from Rebecca. "Our first advertisement."

Rebecca picked up the newspaper, scanning the page until she found the small ad halfway down.

STYLISH SLIPCOVERS!
Looking to update your parlor without spending a fortune?
Go to Macintosh Furniture and Upholstery Co.
Here you will find samples of our stylish slipcovers.
Tailor made from brightly printed cottons,

these covers are a necessity for all households.
Remember — Macintosh Furniture and Upholstery Co. is the only place you need to go.
C. Macintosh & R. Johnson

"R. Johnson." Rebecca frowned and laid the paper back down on the table. "You added my name?"

"Of course. You're the backbone of this venture." Caroline leaned forward and squeezed Rebecca's hand. "What's wrong? You don't look very happy."

"I don't know."

Biting the edge of her lip, Rebecca walked toward the front of the shop. Miniature replicas of ready-made furniture had been artistically arranged among yards of cream and gold silk fabric in front of the window, advertising their goods to everyone who walked by the brick-faced building. Leaning against the top of one of the hand-carved dressers, she stared past the colorful display to the bustle of traffic on the street outside and watched the busy scene unfold before her.

Everyone seemed to have a purpose and direction. Drivers traversed the cobblestone street toward known destinations. Pedestrians weaved carefully through the traffic to their next appointments. Was she the only one who didn't know where her life was headed?

"Do you ever question God's will for you?" Rebecca turned back to Caroline. She wanted to confide in her, but how could she when she didn't understand her own growing dissatisfaction? "I feel so unsure about everything."

"Do you still miss Jake?"

"No." Rebecca blinked back the tears and tried to work through the jumble of emotions so she could explain clearly how she felt. "I miss what we planned together — a home, children."

"You're twenty years old, Rebecca. You've got your whole life ahead of you and a God far bigger than any earthly problem. Trust Him to show you His plan for your life, in His timing."

Rebecca allowed a slight smile to cross her lips. "So you're telling me to have patience?"

"Patience isn't an easy virtue, is it?" Caroline ran her hand across her stomach and let out a soft chuckle. "There was a time when I was convinced it would take a whole lot more than patience to win Philip's heart."

Rebecca paced the length of the shop again, back to where Caroline sat. "What do you mean?"

"I don't know how much Michaela told you, but Philip was once quite smitten with her."

Rebecca's stepmother had told her parts of the story. In the end it had been Eric Johnson, Rebecca's father, who had stolen Michaela's heart. And shortly after that, Philip had discovered Caroline was the one he truly loved. "I guess God does work things together for good."

"And the same is true for you. I believe coming here was God's will for you." Caroline picked up one of the slipcovers Rebecca had just finished and ran her hand across the fabric. "It's giving you time to figure out what you want to do with your life. Look at your work. God has given you an incredible gift. This is absolutely flawless."

"I do enjoy it."

Rebecca reclaimed her chair across from Caroline, smoothing out the silky folds of her Napoleon blue taffeta dress. Maybe this was the direction God had planned for her. She could help Caroline build up her business and maybe even open her own shop one day. Still, if living in Boston was God's will, then why did she feel such a stark

21

emptiness inside? Something was missing, and she knew it wasn't Jake.

Caroline fingered one of her blond tresses. "Since you've been here, business has doubled because of referrals for your work. I may have had the inspiration of combining Philip's cabinetmaking business with the fabric slipcovers, but I'm not near the seamstress you are."

Rebecca dropped her gaze at the compliment. "I don't know about that —"

"It's true." Caroline waved her hand in the air. "Besides, after the baby comes, Philip is insisting I stay home more. I don't know what I'd do without you."

Rebecca smiled. It did feel good to be needed.

Caroline eased out of her chair. "Pretty soon I won't be able to stand without help."

Rebecca grabbed Caroline's hand to help her up and grinned. "Pretty soon you'll be holding your precious son or daughter in your arms."

"I can't wait." A warm, satisfied look swept across Caroline's face. "Which reminds me, I promised Philip I'd rest this afternoon. You don't mind watching the store, do you? Philip will be out back in the workroom if you need anything."

"Of course I don't mind. That's fine."

Caroline picked up the newspaper and pulled it to her chest. "Patience Hutton is supposed to drop by and pick up the rosewood table Philip repaired for her."

Rebecca began folding the leftover pieces of the indigo fabric and setting them in a pile. "He showed it to me this morning. It's beautiful."

"He did a good job. You can't even tell it was broken." Caroline paused at the bottom of the staircase that led to the apartment she and Philip shared above the store. "Have you met Mrs. Hutton yet?"

"I don't believe so."

Caroline leaned against the door frame. "Now there's a woman I'd love for us to get as a client."

"Why's that?"

"Her home is supposed to resemble a museum. She has a collection of silver pieces that have been passed down in her family for five generations, as well as all sorts of family heirlooms."

"How wonderful to be able to pass down treasures like that to your children."

Caroline nodded. "Now it's just her and her son. I believe he builds ships for a living, but the family was in the whaling business for several generations."

Rebecca set the last piece of folded fabric

on the pile. "Did you know my grandfather was the captain of a whaling vessel?"

"Really? I've always thought that would be such a romantic profession."

Rebecca's eyes narrowed. "What's so romantic about waiting years for your husband to return from an expedition? The whaling and fishing industries are all horribly dangerous lines of work. My father once told me of a storm in which thirteen vessels went down carrying about a hundred and fifty fishermen. Think of all the widows and orphans those sailors left behind."

"All right, you have a point." Caroline's hazel eyes sparkled. "I was thinking more about the lovelorn bride waiting anxiously day after day for her husband to return from sea."

"Sounds like a tragedy to me."

"All of Shakespeare's romances ended in tragedy. *Romeo and Juliet* —"

"Enough." Rebecca laughed as she added the entire pile of scraps to the bin that held other bits and pieces of leftover fabric. "You're talking to a girl who only knows a tragic end to romance, unlike your happily-ever-after story with Philip."

"Your day will come, Rebecca. I have no doubt about it."

"Maybe, but for now I plan to leave tales

of romance, tragic or not, to the storytellers."

A warm breeze off the Atlantic seaboard ruffled Luke Hutton's work shirt as he finished greasing the skids beneath the hardwood runners of the schooner he was building. He was eager for the day she would set sail. Boston's shipyards were full of clipper ships, whaling vessels, private yachts, and commercial fishing boats, but this one he was helping to build with his own hands.

Luke gazed out across the harbor and watched the stately crafts bob in the sparkling blue coastal waters. Folding his arms across his chest, he let out a contented sigh. The smell of the ocean permeated the air, and he could taste the salt from the Atlantic on his lips. It was something he couldn't deny. The sea was in his blood.

"She's going to be a fine sailing vessel, young man." Dwight Nevin stepped onto the deck behind Luke, inspecting the work he'd just completed.

"You're right, sir." Luke turned to greet his boss. "She's a beauty."

Working for Dwight Nevin as a ship's carpenter had been a dream come true. In many ways Mr. Nevin was the father figure

Luke had longed for after the death of his own. And he didn't disapprove of Luke saying exactly what was on his mind. Something he was prone to do.

Luke grinned at the redheaded Irishman, who at fifty-five was as fit as any sailor. "I still predict that one day soon the demand for private yachts will overtake commercial boats."

"Never." Mr. Nevin shook his head and frowned, but Luke didn't miss the sparkle in his eyes.

"With all due respect, sir, it's already happening. Summer resorts are bringing in more tourists every year, while the fishing industry is dwindling. We're seeing an increase in land values along the coast as towns are being influenced by the influx of visitors."

The older man waved his hand in front of him. "A few tourists will never make that much of an impact. The entire commercial fishing industry will never die down."

"Like the whaling industry, sir?"

"Okay, you've made your point." Mr. Nevin groaned and started up the narrow wooden plank toward the small building used as an office for the modest shipbuilding company. "Let the tourists have their fun. Fishing's been a way of life for my family for the past four generations. And your family, too. It's in our blood."

"Maybe, but the future isn't in whaling anymore." A seagull cried out above him as Luke hurried to follow his boss up the plank. "We — you — ought to be looking more into the private sector. You could double, triple, your business if you wanted to."

"Business is fine."

"True, but what about tomorrow? Just think about it. Twenty years ago whaling was a highly profitable business, but now kerosene has replaced the need for whale oil and candles."

Mr. Nevin stopped and blew out a labored sigh. "What does your mother think about this?"

"My mother's like you. She refuses to think that things might be changing."

"You're going out again on a whaling expedition, though, aren't you?"

Luke tugged at his shirt collar, sorry for the reminder. It wasn't as if he dreaded the trip. Sailing would always be a part of him, but lately his interest had focused on building the crafts. "I leave in a month. But this will be my last trip."

"Have you told your mother it will be your final voyage?"

"My mother believes it's God's will for me to captain my own vessel someday. So far nothing I have said or done, including working for you, has helped alter what she believes to be true."

"What you need to do is to find yourself a nice girl and settle down."

Luke frowned at the older man. He'd heard the very same comment a dozen times. "What 'nice girl' is going to wait three years for me to come back?"

"Find the right girl, and she'll wait."

Luke scuffed the wooden plank with his boot and shook his head. "Not likely, sir."

"Well, I'll tell you one thing, Luke Hutton. You've got initiative, that's for sure. If you can survive the next few years battling the sea, and if I can survive my wife's constant nagging, when you get back I'll have a job waiting for you."

Two hours later Luke stepped into Macintosh Furniture and Upholstery and breathed in the mixture of cedar, pine, and fresh wood shavings. While building boats was his passion, he'd dabbled with carpentry enough to respect the expertise it demanded. And from what he'd heard, Philip Macintosh's craftsmanship was some of the finest in the area.

28

"May I help you?"

Luke's gaze turned from a skillfully carved table and stopped at the dark-haired beauty who stood in the center of the showroom. "Yes. I'm — I'm here to pick up a table for my mother, Patience Hutton."

Luke took a step backward, annoyed at his sudden awkwardness. What was wrong with him? His boss mentioned he should settle down, and suddenly the next pretty girl he sees is marriage material?

The young woman clasped her hands in front of her. "I was expecting her to come by."

"It was on my way home. I hope it's not a problem."

She laughed then shook her head. "It's not a problem who picks it up. I just meant that we were expecting her this afternoon. The table's ready."

"Good — I know she'll be pleased."

"But you haven't seen the table yet."

Luke cleared his throat. Why was everything he tried to say coming out wrong? "Is there a problem with it?"

"No, but I do want to make sure you're satisfied with the work before you take it."

"Of course."

"If you'll come with me, you can look at it." She headed toward the back of the store, letting him follow. "It's a beautiful piece."

"It's one of my mother's favorites." Luke stopped at the table and ran his fingers across the polished top. "Unfortunately, a recent guest of ours managed to knock it over, cracking the narrow leg."

"That's a shame, but if you take a close look, I don't think you'll even be able to tell where the crack was."

Luke examined the curved leg of the table and smiled. "Excellent work. The wood has been matched to perfection, and the seam is even."

"Do you know a lot about carpentry?"

"Not tables and chairs, per se." Luke rubbed his hands together and caught her gaze. Dark brown eyes stared back at him, and he wondered suddenly what was hidden behind them. He'd heard the laughter in her voice but hadn't missed the unmistakable look of sadness. "I've been working for Dwight Nevin as his apprentice. Right now we're building a fifty-foot, two-masted, rigged schooner."

"For fishing or cargo shipments?"

Luke's eyes widened in surprise at her question. "This one is going to be for fishing. Are you interested in the boating industry?"

A dimple appeared in her right cheek

when she smiled. "My grandfather was the captain of a whaling vessel. While I never knew him, I've always been fascinated by the sea and the stories it has to tell."

"I come from a long line of whalers, as well." For some reason he didn't want their conversation to end. The table was finished. There was nothing holding him here except one thing. "I'm Luke Hutton, by the way."

"Rebecca Johnson." She shook his hand then brushed back a wisp of her coal-black hair. "I'm related to Philip Macintosh by marriage. Actually, it's a bit complicated. He's the brother-in-law of my stepmother."

"So you have a big family?" He picked up the small table and tried to tell himself her answer didn't interest him. But it did.

Rebecca laughed again. "You could say that. Three brothers and two sisters. Then Anna was adopted into our family, making it seven."

Luke let out a low whistle. "I'm an only child. My father passed away, so now it's just me and my mother." He needed to go, but something about her urged him to stay and prolong their talk. "Have you lived here long? I've been in the shop once or twice before. I don't remember ever seeing you."

"I recently moved here from Cranton."

"Cranton." He searched his memory for

information on the small town in western Massachusetts. "That's not too far from the Connecticut River, I believe?"

"Yes. It's a beautiful place. Lush farmland, lazy brooks, apple orchards . . . I loved it there."

He caught the look of sadness in her eyes again. Maybe she was simply homesick. He knew from experience that Boston could be an overwhelming city. Hadn't he felt the same way on his last return from sea? The bustling metropolitan area was a stark contrast to the seclusion of life on deck. And Cranton was nothing more than a sleepy little farming community.

"Would it be too bold if I ask why you left?"

She started for the front of the shop. This time he matched her stride and walked beside her. "Caroline, Philip's wife, decided it might be good for business to expand beyond tables and chairs and start offering custom-made slipcovers to their patrons. Business was growing so quickly that she needed the extra help. I thought Boston would be a nice change."

"Slipcovers?"

Rebecca paused at a well-crafted mahogany sideboard and turned to him. "I know they don't take nearly as much skill as fine furniture, but they do seem to be the rage right now —"

"No, it's a great idea." Luke hoisted the table against his hip. "Expanding on the clientele you already have. In fact, my mother mentioned just last week how she thought slipcovers would be perfect in the parlor."

Her hand traced the carved inlay atop the sideboard. Long, slender fingers. Skin the color of cream —

"You could bring your mother by tomorrow if you'd like," Rebecca said, putting a halt to his wandering thoughts. "I could show her samples of what we can do."

He shouldn't. He should turn and walk out of the shop and forget ever meeting Miss Rebecca Johnson. Instead he caught her gaze and smiled. "That's a wonderful idea."

Luke placed his mother's table carefully in the back of the buggy, all the time wondering why he'd just told Miss Johnson he'd be back. He knew his return had nothing to do with showing his mother samples of slipcovers and everything to do with seeing her again.

He flicked the reins, urging his palomino to hurry home. His last whaling voyage had

taken three and a half years, and considering he was weeks away from departing on
his second trip, it made no sense to pursue
this unexplained — and unwelcome — attraction to Rebecca Johnson.

It simply wasn't possible. Problem was, he
did yearn for a wife and a family. Yet by the
time he returned from sea, he'd be close to
thirty years old — and no closer to marriage than he was now.

Two

Rebecca pulled out another piece of brightly printed cotton and held it up for Patience Hutton to examine. It was the fifth sample she'd shown the older woman in the last hour. Up to this point nothing had been acceptable.

"What do you think about this one?" Rebecca waited as Mrs. Hutton fingered the fabric.

In Rebecca's opinion the color combination was perfect for the stylish parlor. The shades of light green, delft blue, and sunny yellow would make stunning slipcovers without overpowering the classical style of the room.

Rebecca leaned forward on the elegant Grecian sofa, watching the older woman's reaction. She'd been disappointed when, instead of a visit from Luke Hutton, she'd received a message from his mother requesting her to come to their home. No matter how hard she tried, she hadn't been able to forget those penetrating brown eyes that reminded her of the syrup her brother Adam made each winter from his sugar maple trees. Luke's gaze had caused her heart to tremble, something she hadn't expected — or wanted. Still, the thought of seeing the broad-shouldered, muscular shipbuilder again had kept her dreams flavored with the sweetness of his gaze.

Taking the sample of fabric from Rebecca, Mrs. Hutton walked toward the window, smoothing back a loose strand of silver hair that had fallen from the neat pile atop her head. The bustle of her elegant silk dress rustled as she turned to Rebecca and smiled. "This one is perfect."

Rebecca let out a sigh of relief. After arriving at the Hutton home, she'd learned that not only did Patience Hutton have a stunning place as Caroline had told her, but she was also a woman who was hard to please. No doubt keeping her happy throughout the project would be a challenge.

"And what about the windows?" Mrs. Hutton held the fabric up to the light.

Rebecca nodded at the suggestion. "We could easily hang panels from a cornice using the same fabric."

"Simple but elegant. I like that." Mrs. Hutton sat back down on the sofa, still holding the fabric sample. "Funny, something about the colors reminds me of my childhood home. My mother was Dutch, and our home was filled with delft blue pieces of earthenware from Holland."

"I believe I saw several of them in your curio cabinet?"

"Yes." Mrs. Hutton smiled, obviously pleased Rebecca had noticed.

Those decorations hadn't been the only thing Rebecca noted. In a brief tour of the downstairs, she'd studied the numerous pieces of furniture. Most of them, she judged, had been fabricated prior to the Revolution. A Baltimore clock with its fine inlaid design of vines and leaves, a Sheraton-styled secretary with painted-glass panels, and a number of ornately carved tables. The walls were filled with tapestries, portraits of family members, and a number of detailed needlework pieces.

"Have you always lived in Boston?" Rebecca began gathering the samples she'd brought with her, pleased that having chosen the fabric she could begin making the slipcovers.

"I spent most of my life on Nantucket Island. My late husband and I came to

37

Boston only eighteen months before he died. For some reason I've never wanted to move back. Too many memories, I suppose."

Rebecca's eyes widened with interest. "My mother's parents lived their whole lives on Nantucket Island."

"Really? What were their names?"

"Edmund and Margaret Stevens, but only my grandmother is still alive."

Her face beaming with delight, Mrs. Hutton clapped her hands. "I knew your grandparents well when my husband and I lived on the island. In fact, I still stay in touch with your grandmother."

"Unfortunately, when my mother married my father, it caused a rift in the family." Rebecca placed the last square of fabric, a blend of dark purple and gold, into her large tapestry bag. "I haven't seen my grandmother since I was a little girl."

"I admit, she rarely talked about her family but did mention your mother a few times." Mrs. Hutton let out a soft laugh. "I truly am sorry to hear that you never got to know her, but Margaret always was stubborn. To be honest, it doesn't surprise me one bit."

"My mother used to tell me stories of my grandmother's beautiful flower garden and my grandfather's whaling ship, the *Lady Amaryllis*." Rebecca smiled at the memories. "I'd love to hear more."

"I have an idea. Why don't you stay for lunch?" Mrs. Hutton patted Rebecca's hand. "That will give us time to talk. I believe we're having Irish stew."

Thrilled for the opportunity to learn more about her grandparents, Rebecca nodded. "I'd like that. Thank you."

"First, though, come with me. I want to show you something."

Rebecca stood at the window of Mrs. Hutton's bedroom, admiring the view of the blossoming gardens from the large windows while the older woman rummaged through the bottom drawer of the secretary. Massive oak trees rose up from the green earth, tall and proud, their leaves blowing in the soft wind. Flowers spilled across the edges of the manicured lawn, a stunning mosaic of yellows, oranges, pinks, and reds. Inside, the room was like the rest of the house, full of beautiful furniture, thick carpets, and heavy drapes.

With a large folder in her hands, Mrs. Hutton sat on a padded ottoman and motioned for Rebecca to join her. "I don't even remember the last time I looked at these."

"What are they?" Curious, Rebecca sat down beside her.

"My late husband, Isaac, was quite an artist. He never tired of drawing portraits of friends and family." One by one she pulled out the illustrations, each full of remarkable detail.

"Here. This is what I wanted to show you. These are your grandparents."

Rebecca's breath caught in her throat as she took the drawing and held it. "When did he do this?"

"I'd say about twenty-five years ago. I remember this picture in particular. We'd just celebrated your grandmother's fortieth birthday. Isaac sketched this portrait of them in the garden."

Tears welled in Rebecca's eyes as she ran her finger across the bottom edge of the paper. In the hands of a true artist, the charcoal pencil had managed to capture every detail of their expressions — including the mischievous twinkle in her grandfather's eye.

"Grandfather looks as if he's up to something."

Mrs. Hutton laughed. "He always did have that Cheshire grin, and yes, he was a prankster, too. You'd think that being the captain of a whaling ship he'd be a bit more serious, but not your grandfather."

"And my grandmother?" Rebecca studied the drawing that had captured the curves of her full face and the soft curls that framed her hair. "What is she like? She's beautiful in this picture."

"And still is. She was always the serious one, though."

Rebecca looked back to Mrs. Hutton. "Do you know why she cut off contact with my mother?"

"Knowing Margaret the way I do, I'd have to say it was her pride." Mrs. Hutton shook her head slowly. "When your father moved your mother away from the island, it broke her heart. She never learned how to love and let go."

"She sent us a piano for Christmas one winter, thinking it would help us become more cultured." For the first time Rebecca caught a glimpse of what she'd missed all these years, and it filled her with a sense of regret and longing. "I think that was the last time we heard from her. She didn't even come for my mother's funeral."

"If only your grandfather had been alive. He would have talked some sense into her."

"I've thought about going to see her. Nantucket Island's not too far from Boston. I don't know why I've put it off so long."

41

"She's not on the island right now."

Rebecca raised her brows in question. "Where is she?"

"The last time I saw her, she was preparing to leave for England."

"England?" Rebecca frowned. Had she lost her grandmother just when she'd finally realized what she'd been missing?

"Your grandmother came to America when she was only seventeen. She'd always wanted to return to the village in which she grew up."

"When is she coming back?"

"Late fall at the earliest. She promised to contact me on her return."

Rebecca didn't understand a number of things about her parents' relationship with her grandmother. Nevertheless, as soon as she came back from England, she would make a point of visiting her on the island.

Rebecca thumbed through the rest of the drawings, stopping at a picture of a young boy. "Is this Luke?"

"You can tell?" Mrs. Hutton's wrinkled hand touched the edge of the drawing. "He was only seven years old when his father drew this."

"He has the same eyes and dark full brows." Trying to cover her interest, Rebecca turned to the next page. "Luke was a handsome child."

"*Was* handsome?"

Rebecca turned to the doorway at Luke's voice, letting the portrait flutter onto her lap. He stood there, his lips turned into a half grin. Her stomach lurched. Broad shoulders, square jawline, dark, wavy hair. He shouldn't affect her this way. But he did.

"I . . ." Rebecca struggled to regain her composure. "Your mother was just showing me some of your father's drawings. Your parents knew my grandparents on Nantucket Island."

Luke caught her gaze, sending her stomach reeling. "It's quite a small world, isn't it?"

"Your timing is perfect, Luke." Mrs. Hutton smiled at her son as she gathered the pictures. "You can join us for lunch."

Luke's mouth watered as a generous helping of stew was set in front of him. He'd managed to get away for lunch, and after seeing Rebecca again, he wasn't a bit sorry he'd cut his morning's work short. Her yellow dress, shimmering in the midday sunlight that filtered through the large open window, brought out glints of gold in her dark eyes. She wore her hair the same way as the last time he'd seen her, parted in the center and secured at the nape of her neck, with short, curly bangs framing her heart-shaped face.

"Luke? Haven't you heard a word we've said?"

Luke shot his mother a sheepish grin and set his spoon in his bowl. "Sorry, Mother — my mind must have been wandering."

"You spend far too much time thinking about that boat you're building." Mrs. Hutton pressed her napkin to her lips. "Of course I can't complain too much." She turned her gaze to Rebecca. "It's good to have him around. One of these days he'll find himself a good wife, and I'll be wishing he was back."

Luke stifled a laugh, wondering what his mother would say if she knew what he had been thinking. Finding a wife had never been a priority in his life. Not until lately, anyway. Right now he could hardly keep his gaze off the dark-haired beauty seated across the table. Rebecca smiled at him, and Luke looked away, trying to ignore the strange sensation coursing through his veins.

"I was saying how amazing it is that I knew Rebecca's grandparents so well," his mother said, interrupting his thoughts again.

Luke took a sip of his water. "Of course, with both our families in the whaling business, it certainly makes sense that our paths would cross."

Rebecca's cheeks flushed slightly as she turned to him. "Your mother's promised to tell me about my grandparents."

With the main course cleared away, dessert was served. The lemon cake tasted perfect, but at the moment all Luke noticed was Rebecca. The clock in the corner of the dining room chimed two o'clock. He needed to get back to work but instead lingered at the table, laughing at his mother's anecdotes from years gone by.

"What brought about the changes in my grandmother?" Rebecca set her fork down, letting it clink softly against the blue china plate. "The picture you paint of my grandparents is nothing like the one I know. Your descriptions make them seem so happy and full of life."

"Honestly, I don't know." Scooting back slightly from the table, Luke's mother folded her hands in her lap. "I'd always felt rather close to Margaret; then gradually we began to drift apart. I noticed subtle changes at first, and I never knew what started it. I'm thankful that in the past few years our friendship has resumed."

Rebecca stared out the open window, a trace of sadness marking her expression.

"Maybe I'll have that chance someday, as well."

Setting her napkin on the table, Luke's mother stood. "I hate to cut our lunch short, but I am due shortly at the Mills Street Orphanage to speak to Agnes about an upcoming fund-raiser I'm coordinating."

Rebecca smiled, bringing out the now-familiar dimple in her cheek. "Thank you so much for inviting me to lunch, Mrs. Hutton."

"It was a pleasure meeting you, and we'll be sure to do this again soon. Luke, why don't you walk Rebecca home? I know she would appreciate the company."

Rebecca shook her head. "That's not necessary, really. I'm sure you must get back to work."

Luke paused for a moment, wondering if Rebecca was just being considerate or if she really did want him as her escort. Unable to stop himself, he grinned. He certainly wasn't going to throw away a chance to get to know her better. "It's not a problem at all. I'd be delighted."

THREE

Laughing aloud at one of Rebecca's stories about her siblings, Luke permitted himself to glance at her profile as they strolled down the paved walkway. The Atlantic Ocean, its whitecaps spraying as the tides rolled in, spread beyond them to the east, the bustling city to the west. He breathed in the smell of salt water that permeated the air, bringing with it the sense of freedom he always felt when he was near the ocean. Today, though, it wasn't simply the allure of the sea reeling him in.

Catching the smile that fluttered across Rebecca's lips, Luke grinned. There was something about Rebecca that had captured his interest from the moment they met at the furniture shop. While her beauty couldn't be argued, he was well aware there was much more to her than a lovely face. In the short time he'd been around her, he'd seen her intelligence coupled with a sense of wit.

"You really didn't have to walk me back to the shop, though I do appreciate it." Rebecca turned to him briefly, allowing him another peek into her mahogany-shaded eyes. He had no doubt this was a place in which he could get lost if he allowed himself the chance.

"I don't mind, really." He shoved his hands into his pockets. "My mother seems pleased with what you have planned for the parlor."

"It took quite awhile for her to choose which fabric she wanted to use." Rebecca chuckled softly then stopped to gaze across the water, which was sprinkled with dozens of stately vessels. "With that decision made I'll be able to start working."

Motioning toward the northern part of the harbor, Luke pointed out his boss's shipyard. "That's where I'm learning the shipbuilding trade. Dwight Nevin's one of the best."

"What kind of crafts do you build? I believe you mentioned you were currently working on a two-masted, rigged schooner?"

"You have a good memory." Luke grasped the wooden rail beside Rebecca and stared out across the crystal blue water, glad for the opportunity to prolong their walk. "We mainly build commercial cargo and fishing boats, though we have worked on a couple of yachts. I'm trying to convince my boss that the private sector is the way of the future. Not that there won't be a need for the commercial side, of course, but more and more people are pouring money into crafts simply for pleasure."

"Seems a bit extravagant to me."

Luke laughed. "You're exactly right. It's unbelievable what people will spend their money on. Believe it or not, one man had an electrically ventilated dairy built on his yacht where he keeps a cow so he can have fresh milk every morning for breakfast."

Rebecca's eyes widened. "Surely you're joking?"

"Not at all." He smiled, remembering that he'd reacted the same way when first told about the infamous yacht. "Of course, most boats are built to be more practical. Even the private ones."

"I've always thought the ships were so majestic. I think I could stand here for hours, just gazing across the water."

Luke cleared his throat. Before he listened any longer to what his heart was telling him, he needed her to know he was involved in far more than merely building vessels for others to pilot. "Rebecca, there's something I need to tell you —"

"Look at that one. Isn't she beautiful?" Rebecca had turned away from him, missing his last words. The wind tugged at her hair as she pointed at the craft, its white sails blowing in the wind.

"It's a whaling vessel." Luke watched the ship as it headed out to sea, another reminder of his own upcoming voyage. "You'll see fewer and fewer these days than you did twenty or thirty years ago. Soon they'll be nothing more than a reminder of the past."

"That may be true, but there will always be fishermen of one kind or another. Those sailors have such dangerous jobs." Rebecca shuddered despite the warmth of the breeze blowing off the ocean. "I've been thinking a lot about my grandmother. I can't help but wonder if part of the reason she became so cold and distant was because of my grandfather's work. I couldn't imagine living like that. Having to wait, month after month, year after year, for the return of your loved one."

Luke's fingers pressed against the rail. He had planned to tell her the truth, but her words stopped him. No matter how strong the attraction he felt toward her, he was fooling himself to think that anything could come of their newfound friendship. How could he have considered courting her with such little time remaining until his next voyage? And even if she did feel something toward him, he knew now she'd never wait for him. She'd just made that clear.

Turning abruptly on his heels, Luke faced her, forcing a smile. "I'd better get you back to the shop. Mr. Nevin's expecting me at work this afternoon."

Ten minutes later Rebecca stood at the front door of Macintosh Furniture and Upholstery, watching Luke merge into the busy crowd of pedestrians. His friendly but curt good-bye had made her certain something had happened between his mother's home and the shop, but for the life of her she had no idea what. She'd been confused by the sudden change in his demeanor at the waterfront. In fact, up until that point she'd even thought she detected a hint of interest on his part. Maybe she was imagining things.

The bell above the door jingled as Rebecca stepped into the shop, thankful it was empty of customers. She laid her bag of fabric samples on the tailor's bench and sank into one of the chairs. It didn't make sense. Maybe she'd been the only one who'd felt the attraction as they talked about common interests such as baseball, politics, and spiritual matters. Of course, she'd been wrong once before when it came to love and marriage. Was God trying to tell her something again?

Rebecca looked up as Caroline entered the showroom from the back.

"How was your afternoon with Mrs. Hutton?" Caroline asked.

"I thought you were supposed to be taking a nap after lunch."

"I'll be on my way upstairs in a minute. Philip asked me to watch the shop momentarily while he stepped out." She rested her hands across the top of her widening stomach. "You didn't answer my question."

Rebecca pulled the pieces of fabric she'd shown to Mrs. Hutton out of her bag and laid them with the rest of the samples. "It was fine. After about an hour she finally decided on the fabric. It's going to look stunning once it's completed. Then she invited me for lunch."

"Really? That's wonderful. I've heard she's a difficult woman to please. You must have done quite well."

Rubbing the satiny material between her fingers, Rebecca smiled. "Her son ate with us, and the food was wonderful. Irish stew and dumplings —"

"I'm not interested in the menu." Caroline held up her hand and laughed. "What about her son? I have the impression you're leaving out some rather important details to this story."

Rebecca lowered her gaze. The last thing she was interested in at the moment was having a discussion about Luke Hutton. "I'm not leaving anything out."

Caroline sat across from Rebecca and rested her elbows against the table. "And I'm not carrying an extra twenty-five pounds around my waist."

Rebecca laughed but felt the heat rush to her cheeks. "Yes, I met Mrs. Hutton's son, Luke, but it's not an important detail. What is important is that not only does Mrs. Hutton want slipcovers made up for the furniture in her parlor; she wants matching drapes, as well."

Caroline leaned back in her chair. "I'm getting the feeling that Luke is quite good-looking, and you're a tad smitten. Am I right?"

Rebecca let out a low moan. "There's more to men than their looks, Caroline."

"Absolutely, but a handsome face added to the package can't hurt. So is he?"

"Is he what?"

Caroline grinned. "Handsome, of course."

"He's very good-looking." If Rebecca closed her eyes, she knew she would be able to see every detail of his face, from his maple-brown eyes to the slight cleft in his chin. Instead she stared at the swirls of yellows and blues in the fabric in front of her, willing the image to vanish. "He builds ships, as you told me, and for now lives at home with his mother. Most important, though, he has a strong faith and is very active in his church."

"And you discovered all of this over lunch?"

Rebecca pursed her lips. "He walked me to the shop."

"Now the story's getting interesting."

Rebecca rose from the table and began gathering the supplies she would need in the morning. She had to return to the Hutton home and take the measurements for the slipcovers. Then most of the work would be completed right here in the shop — a place where she wouldn't run into Luke again.

"Rebecca . . ."

"The story ends there." Rebecca shrugged her shoulder. "I don't know what happened, but we were standing at the waterfront, looking at the ships, and all of a sudden his whole demeanor changed. I must have said something wrong."

"Surely you're imagining things."

"I don't know about that. But even if I didn't, what if I make another wrong decision again?"

Caroline leaned forward and covered Rebecca's hand with her own. "Just because Jake turned out to be someone other than the man you thought he was doesn't mean the next beau who comes along will be the same."

Rebecca shook her head. "Maybe, but I do know one thing. I don't think I'm ready to risk another broken heart."

Luke slathered the thick slice of bread with butter then rummaged in the icebox for a slab of leftover ham. Moonlight filtered through the kitchen window, leaving shadows dancing along the walls. The clock chimed one, reminding him of what he already knew. He should be in bed sound asleep. Instead he hadn't been able to tame his roaming thoughts, leaving him tense and restless.

His sandwich made, Luke slumped into one of the wooden kitchen chairs and took a bite.

"Luke?"

Dropping his sandwich onto the plate, Luke's gaze shifted to the kitchen doorway. "Mother, I'm sorry if I woke you."

"Couldn't sleep?"

He shook his head. "Not a wink."

"Mind if I join you?" His mother pulled the tie of her silk robe tighter around her waist. "The smell of fresh yeast bread aroused my appetite."

"There's plenty left. You know, your cook is spoiling me."

"Just trying to make up for the bland fare you'll be eating at sea." Luke's mother bustled to the counter and made herself a sandwich before joining him back at the table. "Care to let me take a guess at your problem?"

Picking up a crumb with his forefinger, Luke smiled at his mother. "Take a shot. You always were better at figuring me out than I was."

"Let's see. The first clue would be the way you looked at a certain young woman today over lunch. And if that wasn't enough, the sparkle in your eyes as you left to walk her home is more than enough evidence of a man smitten by the aforementioned woman."

"You sound more like a prosecutor than my mother." Luke let out a long groan. "It's that obvious?"

"To your mother? Yes. To her? I'm not so sure. Though I did notice how flustered she became at your arrival."

Pushing his plate away, Luke rested his elbows on the table. "You know I can't think about courting her — or anyone for that matter."

"Why not? Look at your father and me. We married six weeks from the day we met. A bit shocking to many people, I agree, but sometimes you meet someone and know they're the one. A month later your father left on a three-year voyage."

Luke raked his fingers through his hair. "We stood and watched the boats in the harbor on the way to the shop. She mentioned how she couldn't imagine waiting for someone she loved to return from sea."

"So you never told her you're a whaler?"

"I was going to. Then she started talking about how dangerous the profession is. Instead of telling her the truth, I told her I needed to get her back to the shop."

"I like her, Luke. A lot. But that doesn't mean she's the one for you. The sea is in your blood, and you're going to have to find someone who feels the same way. Someone who will allow you to be who you are."

But is that who I am, Lord?

Luke shook his head. "You're right, Mother. It is in my blood, but that doesn't mean I'm going to spend the rest of my life at sea. I want a family someday. And not one I have to leave behind for years at a time."

"The right girl will wait for you. I waited for your father during each of his voyages, never regretting my decision to marry him."

Luke sighed. He'd heard the stories many times of how his mother had kept busy, counting the months that went by at his grandmother's bakery, while his father sailed the world. That wasn't the life he wanted. He was committed to the next voyage and aimed to keep his word to Captain Taft, but after that he was going to retire from sea life. Whether Rebecca would still be around when he returned . . . that was a whole other question.

FOUR

Only two weeks left.

Luke took in a deep breath of humid air and sighed at the somber thought. The ocean, with its green and blue hues, spread out beside him like a well-polished gem. Gulls glided above the sparkling waters in search of their morning prey. Boats bobbed along ripples that moved across the surface of the sea, some of their occupants likely seeking a day's wage in a good catch, others seeking pleasure beneath the warm sun.

Captain Taft would set sail out of this very harbor in a mere fourteen days, yet for Luke the call to stay ashore grew stronger by the hour. And it was all because of the woman who had unexpectedly entered his life — and perhaps a corner of his heart. Rebecca Johnson happened to be everything he'd imagined he could want in a wife. But the timing couldn't be worse.

He'd managed to see her often these past

couple of weeks. While she worked on slipcovers and draperies, he'd found excuses to stop by the furniture shop with various messages from his mother regarding the decorating project or found ways to be at home while Rebecca worked. And he'd never been disappointed with a moment of their time together. He felt himself drawn to so many things about her. Not only was she pretty and intelligent; she was hardworking, conscientious . . . and he was leaving.

Something he still hadn't told her.

Unlike his father, he could never rush into a relationship, marry, then leave on another voyage. He would never be able to leave behind a family while he went away for years at a time merely to bring home a ship full of cargo that would add to the country's supply of lamp oil, candles, medicines, and perfumes. The call of the sea might be in his blood, but he saw no reason to be a whaler simply because his father was a whaler. Whatever the realities of the situation he knew to be true in his head, his heart couldn't shake the draw he felt to get to know Rebecca better despite the short time he had left.

The piercing cries of street vendors broke into his thoughts. The rancid smell of fish from a fishmonger's cart filled his nostrils. Carriages, wagons, and traps congested the street beside him. Pedestrians hurried along the storefronts. Escaping this hubbub of activity was one reason he loved the ocean's solitude. The peace and quiet he found there made up for the backbreaking work and long hours — but even the lure of the sea never completely took away the deeper loneliness he felt. The endless expanse of water could never give him the cherished relationship between a man and a woman.

"Please, mister, 'ere's a beauty."

Luke stopped in front of a street vendor, a little girl selling small bouquets of colorful flowers. She was clothed in filthy rags, her hair oily and matted; it seemed the beautiful, sweet-smelling arrangement had fared better than she. Normally he never noticed the street vendors who spent their days hawking. Selling everything from newspapers to cheese, oysters to peanuts, pies to bottled water, these vendors were simply a part of the city's bustling backdrop with their shrill cries, blowing of tin horns, or tinkling of bells.

For some reason the pinched, haunted look on the girl's face made him take a closer look. He'd spent the noon hour sampling delicious fish chowder with vegetables and sweet bread pudding for dessert, served by his mother's cook. This girl had more than likely eaten nothing but a slice of bread all day, if that.

Luke reached into his pocket and pulled out a few coins. "What's your name?"

The tousled-haired little girl's eyes widened at the question. Instead of answering, she held up one of the bouquets. "Only twenty cents, mister."

He counted out the money then repeated the question.

The girl's head lowered as she handed him the bouquet. "Mandie."

Luke counted out another twenty cents and handed it to the girl. "Mandie, I want you to find yourself something good to eat tonight."

Before she could object, Luke stuffed the money in her sweaty palm and hurried away. Something should be done about the conditions of children like Mandie, who had to work long hours on the streets for mere pennies. Within five minutes the brick-faced building housing Macintosh Furniture and Upholstery stood before him, and he'd all but forgotten the little street vendor.

Humming quietly to herself, Rebecca finished stitching the hem of the drapery panel that would soon grace the window of Patience Hutton's parlor. Slipcovers adorned the two sofas and matching chairs, and the effect was stunning. Tomorrow Rebecca would hang the curtains, and the room's new décor would be complete. Mrs. Hutton had told Rebecca she was pleased with her work. So pleased, in fact, she'd mentioned the possibility of Rebecca's redecorating the sitting room and Mrs. Hutton's bedroom as well.

Placing the scraps of extra fabric in the already full bin, Rebecca ran her hand through the pile of material whose various patterns now enhanced parlors all over Boston and contemplated the idea that had been forming in her mind throughout the morning. She held up one of the fabric scraps she'd used from Mrs. Hutton's green, blue, and yellow slipcovers and smiled, imagining the vivid colors brightening the beds inside the Mills Street Orphanage. Yes. Her idea would work. It might take a bit of coordinating with some of the women at church, but she had no doubt Caroline and maybe even Mrs. Hutton would be eager to get involved with the worthwhile venture.

To finish the project before the cold Boston winter set in, she'd have to work longer hours to complete not only Mrs. Hutton's work but also the work for the half dozen other clients for whom she was currently commissioned to make slipcovers. But her time would be well spent.

Rebecca glanced up as the bell over the front door of the shop rang, announcing a customer. She drew in a quick breath as Luke, wearing a crisp shirt and coffee-colored trousers, made his way through the row of furniture toward the tailor's bench where she sat surrounded by bolts of colorful fabric.

"Good morning, Rebecca."

"Luke. What a pleasant surprise."

Rebecca smiled, noting the sparkle in his eyes, and hoped this unannounced visit truly was a pleasant occasion for him, as well. This wasn't the first time in the past couple of weeks Luke had dropped by the store unexpectedly with a message for her from his mother. His last visit came with an invitation to his mother's sixtieth birthday party, which would be held at the Hutton home the following evening. Still, if she were to guess, she was quite sure most of the reasons behind his visits were purely concocted as excuses to see her. It was a thought that left her smiling inwardly despite the fact that she had no intentions of letting her feelings for Luke go any further than the friendship they now shared. Jake had done more than enough to cause her to think twice about falling in love again.

Luke's tall, muscular figure towered over her, and she noticed the sharp contrast between the white shirt he wore and his skin, perfectly tanned from hours spent in the shipyard. As much as she wanted to fight it, she couldn't help the flutter of butterflies his presence evoked.

She let out a soft sigh and frowned for an instant. Hadn't Jake's presence once set her heart to trembling, as well? She wasn't one of those empty-headed girls who simply fell for every boy who paid attention to her. No, as much as she liked Luke, she had no guarantees he wasn't as capable of breaking her heart as Jake had been. Jake had been so caught up in himself that he'd never noticed what she needed, and she had no intentions of repeating that same mistake. Besides, once she finished working for Mrs. Hutton, more than likely she'd never see Luke again.

He pulled a bouquet of flowers from behind his back then leaned against a mahogany side table that smelled like the fresh beeswax that had been used on the surface to bring out the shine in the wood.

"I met the saddest-looking little street vendor on my way here today, and, well" — Luke tugged on his ear then handed her the flowers — "I thought you might like these."

"They're beautiful. Thank you." Rebecca took the bouquet and brought it to her face, drawing in the sweet scent of the buds while smiling at his awkward attempts to woo her. Luke Hutton, with all his family wealth and social position, was acting like a flustered schoolboy. Regardless of her hesitations, she had to admit she found his uncertainty endearing.

She stood then crossed the room to one of the cabinets in the back and fished out an empty vase for the flowers before setting them down on her workbench. "I've always thought it's a pity those poor children have to work such long hours for so little."

"I agree, but what's to be done?"

"I have an idea." She hadn't meant to share her thoughts with anyone until she'd worked out the details, but now that she'd begun, maybe it wasn't such a bad thing to get Luke's insight. "It's not a solution for the young street vendors of the city, but rather the Mills Street Orphanage."

"I'd like to hear your idea." He sat down on the other side of her workbench and rested his elbows against the table.

She fumbled with the flowers, trying to arrange them in the vase, which was slightly too big for the bouquet. With all the other vases being used as displays to complement the furniture, she'd have to make it work.

"Before I tell you my idea, would you like some tea?"

Luke tilted his head slightly. "Don't you think it's a bit too hot for tea?"

"For hot tea, certainly. I meant iced tea." Rebecca let out a soft giggle. "Ever since I arrived in Boston, I've developed quite an affinity for drinking tea, both hot and iced. Caroline's the one who got me into the habit, and now, no matter what the weather, I don't think a day goes by without my having at least one glass of tea using Mrs. Lincoln's recipe."

Luke blinked. "Who's Mrs. Lincoln?"

"The author of a recently published cookbook. It's titled *Mrs. Lincoln's Boston Cook Book: What to Do and What Not to Do in Cooking.* It's said to be an instant success. Her recipe for tea, for example, is exceptional. Have you ever been to the Atlantic & Pacific Tea Company?" She tidied up the bits of thread and scraps of fabric on the table, continuing her monologue. "They sell all those little bins of tea from around the world, and I plan to sample each one eventually. It's far more refreshing than tea cakes or bread pudding, which I'm not terribly fond of anyway, although I do admit that peppermint cakes are my weakness and always tempt me —"

Rebecca stopped. She was beginning to sound more like her younger sister Sarah, who never seemed to know when to stop talking, than a grown woman. What interest, if any, would Luke have in peppermint cakes and the A & P Tea Company? On one level she'd grown to feel quite at ease around the eye-catching shipbuilder, but the way he was looking at her now, with his handsome visage, made her heart quiver. And she had the bad habit of talking too much when she was nervous.

"I myself love bread pudding." Luke smiled and let out a low chuckle. "Had some for lunch today, in fact. Next time you come visit our home, though, I'll be sure to tell Mother you prefer peppermint cakes over ordinary tea cakes."

Rebecca pushed back a wisp of her bangs and felt her cheeks warm at his teasing. "It's really not necessary, considering the fact that when I'm there I'll be working."

"You won't be working tomorrow night now, will you? You're coming to my mother's birthday party."

"Yes, of course." While she'd truly come to enjoy Mrs. Hutton's company, she wasn't sure how she would feel attending the rather formal celebration. Festivities back home in Cranton had consisted of homemade cakes and pies, along with savory dishes prepared by hardworking farmwives. She was sure this party would be a far cry from roasting meat on a spit or playing baseball in the pasture behind the family barn.

"Good — I'm glad you're coming. And tell me something else, Miss Rebecca Johnson," Luke said, leaning forward, "what else do you like besides the A & P Tea Company's vast selection of teas, Mrs. Lincoln's recipes, and peppermint cakes?"

Rebecca gnawed on her bottom lip and regarded Luke. Surprisingly, she saw no hint of amusement at her expense in his expression. Only genuine interest as he waited for her response. Convinced it would be better to keep the atmosphere light rather than risk the possibility of their conversation becoming too personal, Rebecca laid her finger against her chin, squinted her eyes, and pretended to think hard over the question. While Luke's attraction to her was becoming obvious, she felt certain she wasn't ready for any declarations from him wanting to call on her formally.

"Let's see. I love corned beef, mashed potatoes, my brother Adam's maple syrup — though not together — and baking just about anything. I dislike seafood and eggnog —"

"Being a man of the sea, I can tell you that you don't know what you're missing when it comes to seafood."

She folded her arms across her chest and wrinkled her nose. "I know perfectly well what I'm missing, and besides, you've interrupted me. I wasn't finished with my list."

"Please do continue." Luke's satisfied grin told her he was thoroughly enjoying their exchange.

"I can tolerate corn chowder, which I know I should love along with the seafood, being a favorite Massachusetts fare, and I do love baseball, which doesn't exactly fit into the food category, but I like it all the same."

"That's quite a list."

Rebecca took a deep breath and sat down across from him, hoping she hadn't rambled too much this time and made an utter fool out of herself. "What about you?"

"Well, I suppose I'm rather easy to please when it comes to the subject of food. I have a bit of a sweet tooth, being rather fond of things like the aforementioned bread pudding, and then there's pumpkin pie, apple pie, and cherry pie. Any pie or cake for that matter, I suppose."

"And shipbuilding?"

"Now you're interrupting me." He shot her an amused look. "I also like boats, sailing, and baseball, and I'm rather good at chess."

Rebecca glanced at the front door and, for the first time all day, wished a customer would interrupt them. It was becoming far too difficult to stop the growing attraction she felt toward the young man sitting across from her.

Luke cleared his throat. "Enough about me. You never told me your idea for the Mills Street Orphanage. I'd like to hear it."

Rebecca paused. Jake had rarely shown interest in things she was concerned with. Not that he'd been totally indifferent toward her, but looking back, she realized their conversations had focused primarily on his work and his interests.

"After my father married my stepmother, Michaela, our family adopted my youngest sister, Anna." Rebecca closed her eyes for a moment and smiled at the image of the little girl's face. While the first few months had been somewhat of an adjustment for her, she was now as much a part of the family as any of the Johnsons' other six children. "Anna lost her parents in a terrible fire and ended up living at the orphanage for a couple of years. After hearing her story and realizing the important role the orphanage played in her life, I've wanted to get involved and do something to help make the children's lives better."

Rebecca reached for the large box of scraps and pulled out a handful. "For the past eight months I've been paid to make slipcovers and drapes of every color imaginable. There are at least four more boxes like this in the back. My clients don't want them, but for some reason I've never gotten rid of them. Now I know why."

"Something regarding your idea to help the Mills Street Orphanage?"

Rebecca nodded. "I propose to get a group of women together and with this fabric make quilts for the orphans for this coming winter."

"That's a great idea."

She smiled at his encouragement but wished his enthusiastic compliment didn't affect her as much as it did. "It's a simple idea, really, and I don't know why I didn't think of it earlier. It's easy to give money or old clothes away, but I wanted to do something with my talents that would help me actually get involved in the lives of the children. I want to help each child pick out the colors for his or her quilt, so it's something special that's theirs."

"That makes your idea even better." Luke leaned back in his chair, his expression serious. "Though I'm afraid I'm guilty on that account."

Rebecca wrinkled her brow. "What do you mean?"

"Take, for instance, the street vendor I bought the flowers from. I gave her an extra twenty cents to buy something to eat, but that's a far cry from getting involved in someone else's life and making a difference. Giving money, while important, is easy. Looking into the face of one of the street children and becoming a part of their lives takes things to an entirely different level. And by the way, you need to talk to my mother about your idea. I have a feeling she'll want to get involved."

"Thanks." Rebecca smiled. "I'd planned to."

Luke stood up from the bench then stretched his arms behind him. "I hadn't intended to stay long. In fact, I don't think I ever told you why I came by."

"No, you didn't." A small part of her

wondered if he had come by to ask her if he could call on her in a more formal manner. And a small part of her suddenly longed for him to do so. Could she dare allow herself to daydream about the possibility of a future with him? A home surrounded by a beautiful garden, children . . .

"My mother wanted to make sure you could still come by early in the morning to finish hanging her draperies in time for the party."

Rebecca swallowed her disappointment. "Please tell your mother I've finished the panels and plan to hang them in the morning."

Who was she to think that Luke Hutton, a sophisticated Bostonian from a well-to-do family, would be interested in her, a simple farm girl?

"Good. Then if I don't see you before tomorrow night at my mother's party, I'll look forward to seeing you then."

Rebecca watched as Luke stepped out the door into the morning sunlight. The whole situation was ridiculous. Obviously his visits meant nothing more to him than the fact that he was passing on messages from his mother. It was all business. She glanced at the flowers and ran her fingers across one of the soft petals. And the bouquet, of course, was nothing more than an attempt to help a poor little street vendor. His actions showed he had a heart for the down-and-out, not an interest in her. All the same she had the distinct feeling that if Luke Hutton ever did ask permission to come calling, she'd say yes without a moment's hesitation.

He had to tell her. How he could have let things go this far, he wasn't sure. Of course, it wasn't as if he'd officially asked if he could call on her. He'd come close to asking her several times, but what respectable man in his position would dare act on his desires? And he had no idea how she felt about him. Did she share his interest, realizing his frequent visits to the shop stemmed from contrived excuses to see her? Or were her friendly conversation and bright smile simply the way she dealt with all her clients? Either way, she had to know he was leaving. He'd see her tomorrow at his mother's party, and somehow he'd find the courage to tell her the truth.

FIVE

Rebecca stood in front of the beveled mirror in the upstairs bedroom of Aunt Clara's home and gazed intently at her reflection. The invitation to Mrs. Hutton's birthday party gave her an opportunity to wear the gown she'd made for herself from one of Caroline's paper patterns. The emerald green satin hung gracefully from her waist with a fashionable tier of frills down the back. Her mother's hair ornament, with its glimmering rhinestones shaped like a butterfly, made the perfect finishing touch.

Letting out a deep sigh, Rebecca chastised herself for taking extra pains over her appearance tonight. Luke obviously wasn't going to ask if he could call on her, despite the number of opportunities that had arisen the past few days. He was simply charming, generous, handsome . . . and loved bread pudding. Period. More than likely she had run him off with her incessant babbling over

Mrs. Lincoln's iced tea and how much she loved peppermint cakes. Didn't the basic rules of etiquette state clearly that ladies should avoid talking too much?

She hadn't considered what Luke Hutton thought about her until he looked at her with his dreamy eyes and lopsided smile. Trying to catch hold of her emotions, she worked to straighten the wide satin ribbon at her waist. For a moment she wished she were back home in Cranton. She missed her family. Missed the gray-shingled farmhouse surrounded by lush acres of farmland, apple orchards, and stately elms.

Not that Boston wasn't a fascinating city. She'd come to enjoy the constant bustle of activity, as well as the contrasting majesty of the Atlantic Ocean. Still, she missed her younger sister Sarah's laughter and her brothers, with Adam's gentle teasing and Samuel's stories stemming from his sense of adventure.

A sharp rap on the door jarred Rebecca from her somber thoughts. Aunt Clara entered the room with a bright smile on her sweet, wrinkled face.

"I'm almost ready," Rebecca said.

Aunt Clara waved her hand. "Ben just arrived home and won't be ready for another few minutes, so you're fine." She glanced in the mirror and pushed back a silver wisp of her hair, which was complemented by her olive-colored dress, then chuckled softly. "He's not a bit pleased that I'm making him wear a dinner jacket to Patience's party tonight."

Rebecca couldn't help but laugh, knowing very well how opposed he was to formal attire. "You know Uncle Ben would do anything for you. He adores you."

After two and a half years of marriage, the older couple still acted like newlyweds. Rebecca frowned at the sudden thought of marriage and newlywed bliss. She still had no regrets over stopping her own nuptials, but the longing for marriage and a family still compelled her — almost as much as it frightened her.

Aunt Clara smoothed down the folds of her dress with the palms of her hands and eyed Rebecca intensely. "Why the sad look all of a sudden?"

Rebecca sat on the cream-colored quilt her grandmother had made years before. "I'm a bit homesick, I suppose."

"Did something happen?"

"Not really." Nothing more than foolish daydreams about a handsome shipbuilder. Hadn't she learned her lesson about love once before? But Luke seemed so different. . . .

"Then I believe that tonight is the perfect remedy for your doldrums." Aunt Clara reached out to adjust Rebecca's hair clip. "There's nothing like a party to lift one's spirits."

Rebecca's lips curled into a slight smile. "I suppose you're right. I've always loved parties."

"And you look beautiful. I'm quite certain you'll capture the eye of at least one or two young gentlemen this evening."

Rebecca shivered. "I think I'd prefer to be a simple wallflower than attract the attention of some interested suitor."

"Plenty of young men regard marriage in a higher light than Jake did, you know."

"Yes, but if a man is always going to add such complications to my life, I don't know if I ever want to get married."

"The right man is worth the extra complication." Aunt Clara rested her hands against her hips and tilted her head. "Who is it?"

"Who is it?" Rebecca started at the question. Surely her unsolicited yet seemingly irrepressible interest in Luke hadn't been obvious. "It's no one. No one important, anyway."

"Luke Hutton, by any chance?"

Rebecca felt her cheeks flush at the mention of Luke's name. "How did you know?"

Aunt Clara rested her forefinger against her chin. "Let's see. If I recall correctly, his name has been mentioned at least once over dinner most nights, and —"

"I was simply — simply sharing with you the events of my day." Rebecca stumbled over her excuse. "He often dropped by to leave messages from his mother regarding the work I'm doing for her. Nothing more." *Nothing more intended on his part, that is.*

"And that's the other thing," Aunt Clara began with a twinkle in her eye. "How many of your other clients require a personal carrier to deliver messages to you regarding their slipcovers and draperies?"

"None, but —" Rebecca closed her mouth, feeling caught.

"I've known his family for years, and he's a good man." Aunt Clara reached out and squeezed Rebecca's hands. "Take your time and get to know him. Maybe something will come of it. On the other hand, maybe he'll never be more than a good friend. Just don't let the past stop you from finding out."

Rebecca stood and wrapped her arms around the older woman's waist. If only forgetting the past could be easier. Still, she knew Aunt Clara was right. She'd never find out what could happen between her and

Luke, or any other man, if she let Jake's actions stop her from trusting her heart again. "I know why Michaela loves you so much. She told me how wise you are."

"I'm just an old woman who's thankful to have been blessed by love twice in a lifetime."

Rebecca closed her eyes and wondered if she had any chance at all to find true love — just once.

Classical music played in the background as Rebecca sipped the tangy citrus- and tea-flavored punch from a crystal cup. A number of elegantly dressed guests mingled along the outskirts of the room, but for the moment Rebecca enjoyed studying her surroundings. Mrs. Hutton had chosen to hold the party in a large room that led to the outside terrace and well-manicured gardens below. Like the rest of the house, the room held a collection of fine furniture: rosewood tables with carved grape motifs and marble tabletops, chairs with balloon-shaped backs, and a sideboard with ivory inlay. A pair of gas chandeliers, with cut-glass prisms, reflected dancing shadows on the pale pink wallpaper and added to the festive ambiance of the evening.

Across the room Aunt Clara and Uncle

Ben stood talking to Mrs. Hutton beside a table laden with corned beef, seafood, pies, and other tempting delights. The gracious hostess had greeted Rebecca warmly at the door, but she'd yet to catch a glimpse of Luke. She scanned the room and tried to convince herself it didn't matter if she had the chance to speak to Luke tonight. Surely he'd be far too busy playing host for his mother to pay any attention to her. Regardless of the fact that their families had been longtime friends, she was, in reality, only someone his family had hired. But her heart felt different. She did want to see Luke tonight. Wanted him to seek her out and make her heart quiver the way it did when he was near.

Spotting a friend from church across the room, Rebecca edged past an arrangement of shelves filled with a number of pieces of glassware, framed daguerreotypes, and other unique curios, then stopped at the light touch of someone's fingers against her elbow.

"You look lovely tonight, Rebecca."

Turning slowly, she found herself facing the object of her daydreams. "Luke?"

"I'm sorry if I startled you —"

"No, it's just that —" *It's just that I can't seem to stop thinking about you, and now here you are.*

Her heart fluttered out of rhythm. This time her nervousness left her uncharacteristically tongue-tied. Clean shaven and elegant in his matching charcoal-gray coat, vest, and trousers, he looked as if he'd come straight from the tailor rather than from a day's work at the shipyard.

Luke cleared his throat. "Do you like the punch?"

Rebecca stared at her empty glass. "Yes. It's quite refreshing."

The corners of his eyes crinkled in amusement. "I believe the recipe comes from Mrs. Lincoln's *What to Do and What Not to Do in Cooking.*"

"And I believe you're teasing me." She felt her cheeks flush, something that was becoming too frequent when in Luke's presence.

"Far from it." He stared back at her. "You have an unreserved passion about everything that goes on around you, from Mrs. Lincoln's recipes to things of much weightier importance, like the quilts you're making for the orphans. You know my mother's eager to get involved with the project."

If she'd been the delicate type of female, she was sure she would have swooned by now. Could it be that her instincts were correct and Luke Hutton was interested in her?

Another man, with bright red hair and dressed as elegantly as Luke, stepped up behind him and slapped him on the back. "Luke, why haven't you introduced me to your beautiful companion?"

Luke flashed his friend a look of amusement. "Rebecca, this is Raymond Miller. He's an old — and ornery, might I add — friend of the family."

"Shameful, isn't he? And a pity for you, Luke, that the *Liberty* leaves in a mere two weeks," Raymond said with a wide grin. "I don't suppose I could steal her away for the next dance now, could I?"

Before Rebecca could come up with an excuse to decline the invitation graciously, Luke grasped her forearm lightly with his fingers and drew her toward the dance floor. "Not a chance, sailor."

The music stopped then, and Luke placed her empty cup on one of the tables. "Shall I have the honor of dancing the next waltz with you?"

"Of course." She smiled at his protective manner.

Before she could take another breath, she was in his arms and floating across the room. For a man who worked with his hands and spent most of his time outdoors, he was an excellent dance partner. The intent way he looked down at her left her with no more doubts about his intentions. Clearly he wasn't simply being polite.

Luke rested his gloved hand lightly against Rebecca's waist and breathed in the sweet scent of her perfume. He'd promised himself one dance with her before telling her the truth about his upcoming voyage — before he was caught up even further by her charms. Unfortunately, he was fully aware he had already lost his heart to her.

While the small orchestra played the three-quarter tempo piece, Luke kept his gaze focused on Rebecca. At least a dozen other eligible young women were in the room, each dressed in their finest silks and many showing obvious interest in his status as a wealthy bachelor. But for now Rebecca had his full attention. Despite the fact that etiquette required that he mingle with the other guests throughout the evening and avoid dancing with the same partner, he planned to find a way to prolong their time together.

"Whose idea was this party?" Light from the chandeliers caught the flecks of gold in Rebecca's eyes as she posed the question.

"Originally the idea was mine." Luke drew her slightly closer. "My mother would never have arranged something like this for herself. I'd wanted to surprise her with a few friends over, but those friends, deciding it was a wonderful idea, took matters into their own hands. Before I knew it, half of Boston had been invited."

Rebecca's soft laugh chimed like one of his mother's crystal pieces. "And the surprise part?"

Luke grinned. "Mother found out about it weeks ago. It's impossible to keep a secret from her."

"Why is it that mothers never seem to miss a single detail of what's going on around them?"

The musical piece would come to an end soon, and he knew he had to talk to her. Ignoring the reality of the situation wouldn't change anything. In fact, it would only make matters worse. He'd realized that when he'd introduced her to Raymond, who'd almost given the situation away when he brought up the *Liberty.* He was thankful he'd been able to distract her by asking her to dance. She'd never forgive him if she found out the truth from someone else. And he'd already waited far too long to tell her.

Still, his heart told him to pull her closer

in his arms and beg her to wait for him until he returned. But he'd never do that to her. If only things were different and he wasn't leaving. If only he wasn't facing months of solitude at sea without the sweetness of her face to brighten his day.

"Rebecca, there's something I need to talk to you about. I was wondering if we could stroll in the garden for a few minutes."

Her eyes widened. With interest? He hoped so.

"You're the host tonight. What if your guests need you?"

"I'm sure they can spare me for a few minutes."

"All right, then."

Rebecca took Luke's arm and let him escort her across the floor. With scores of beautiful women filling the room, she couldn't help but feel a thrill that he wanted to spend time with her. And a walk in the garden meant he wanted to prolong their time together. Aunt Clara had been right in her advice. Rebecca couldn't let what Jake had done stop her from finding love again. It was certainly too early to know if Luke was the one God had chosen for her, but it was time to take a chance and find out.

And if he wants to ask if he can call on me

formally . . . Rebecca glided beside him toward the open terrace doors and smiled at the thought of getting to know him better.

An older woman, dressed in a fashionable navy and cream pin-striped silk, stood in the breezeway and greeted them with a pleasant smile. "Luke, darling, let me compliment you on the party. What a wonderful occasion this is for your mother."

"Thank you, Mrs. Lewis. May I introduce you to Rebecca Johnson. Her grandparents have been longtime friends of my mother."

"So you're the young lady in the room who has managed to steal the attentions of our host."

"Knowing Mr. Hutton the little that I do, I'm certain he will strive to make everyone feel at home tonight." Rebecca laced her fingers together, unsure of how else to respond to the woman.

"Don't worry, my sweet. Just be sure to enjoy his company before he leaves."

"Excuse me?" Confused, Rebecca turned to Luke, whose face had paled whiter than a Boston winter.

"Luke," Mrs. Lewis continued, "don't tell me you haven't yet informed this young woman that you set sail in a few days."

Rebecca stood speechless at the announcement, and Luke didn't seem to be faring any better if she was reading correctly the horror-struck expression on his face.

"We're all proud of him. As one of the top officers of the *Liberty,* he's destined to become the captain of his own vessel one day."

Rebecca choked out an unladylike cough. Luke was leaving on a whaling voyage? Surely this woman was incorrect. Luke would have told her something as significant as the fact he was leaving on such an extended expedition. Wouldn't he?

"I hadn't yet . . ." Luke stuttered out his reply. "I was planning on telling her everything now . . . in the garden."

So it was true. He was leaving and had never intended for their relationship to continue.

"If you'll excuse me, I —" The room began to swirl around Rebecca, and her stomach clenched as she ran onto the terrace and into the night air.

Six

Rebecca knew she shouldn't care. Shouldn't care that Luke Hutton was leaving on a whaling voyage that would take him away from Boston for the next three years. Shouldn't care that she'd more than likely never see the handsome sailor again. And why should she? She'd known him a mere few weeks, and in all that time he'd never spoken of his interest in her or said he wanted to call on her. He had no claims on her, nor did she on him.

But he still ought to have told her. How could she dismiss the look in his eyes as he held her in his arms tonight? She'd been so sure of his intentions. Now she knew how wrong she'd been. She was nothing more than another pretty face to him. Someone who could amuse him with animated conversation and other such pleasantries before he had to run off to sea without any thoughts to the future or further commitment. He'd poured on the charm, never once caring that she'd lost her heart in the process.

Drawing back into the shadows of the garden to gain a few moments of privacy, Rebecca took in a deep breath. The sweet scent of the rosebushes did nothing more than remind her of what she'd carelessly dared to dream of having with Luke. A house with a garden, a family . . . How could she have been such a fool to lose her heart again?

And no doubt that was exactly how he saw her — a fool who had misinterpreted his intentions. Didn't Luke Hutton have the choice of every girl here tonight? Their mothers were inside right now, plotting how to get him to notice their little darlings, their sights set on his substantial inheritance. What were a few years of waiting when it came to marrying into a good family with financial stability?

She, on the other hand, had no intention of waiting for months on end for someone like Luke. She wasn't the kind of woman who would pine like a lovelorn maiden for her sweetheart's return — that is, if he'd ever had any plans to ask her, which he obviously hadn't.

"Rebecca?"

She leaned into the flora at the sound of Luke's voice. She should never have run away from him. What kind of undignified behavior had she displayed? Fleeing his mother's party and hiding in the garden were certainly not the actions of a proper lady and only showed him she cared for him. Her heart, though, wasn't acting in a rational manner tonight. Her heart was breaking.

"Rebecca, are you there?"

Swallowing her pride, she knew facing him would be wiser in the long run. "Luke —"

Something pulled against the back of her bustle as she tried to take a step toward him.

"Before you say anything" — he stepped in front of her — "I need to apologize about what happened inside. There are some chairs on the terrace where we could sit, and I could explain —"

"I can't —" Momentarily distracted, she struggled in the dim light to discover what her dress was caught on.

"I never meant for things to turn out this way." He reached forward and brushed his fingers down her sleeve. "I never meant to fall in love with you."

She jerked to face him and heard the ripping of fabric behind her. "You're in love with me?"

Luke was proclaiming his love for her, and she was stuck in the bushes. Of all times for something ridiculous like this to happen. "I think my dress is caught on a thorn — if you could help me."

"Of course."

He reached around to unhook her bustle from the cluster of roses. He was so close she could smell the woodsy scent of his cologne and feel his warm breath against her neck. She tried to steady her rapid pulse. This couldn't be happening. Just when she had decided to take a chance with her heart, she discovered he was leaving. Was it true he wasn't the cad she'd assumed him to be and he really loved her?

"I'm afraid your dress is torn slightly." He picked up a perfect red rose that had fallen to the ground and, after breaking off the thorns, handed it to her.

"Thank you." With the rose in one hand, she stepped into the silvery light of the moon to inspect the garment, but a tear in her dress seemed insignificant at this point. "It's only the bustle and shouldn't be that noticeable."

"Perhaps I shouldn't have spoken so openly," he began, "but I meant what I said. I didn't think it would happen, but you've captured my heart."

She squeezed her eyes shut for a moment and tried to make sense of her jumbled emotions. "I — I don't know what to say."

"Tell me you feel something, too?"

A woman's shrill laugh erupted from the terrace, competing with the soft strains of a violin. Snippets of conversation floated past them. Dogs barked in the distance. Crickets chirped. Each sound gained intensity in her mind, throwing her normally organized thoughts into further confusion.

She wanted to ignore his question, but she couldn't. "How can I let myself continue to care for you now that I know you're leaving?"

"So you feel it, too."

Picking up the hem of her dress, Rebecca escaped toward the terrace. Being alone in the shadows of the garden wasn't proper. And besides, she wasn't sure she could handle his nearness. Not when she knew how much he affected her — and what it meant to her heart to know he was leaving.

She chose a padded bench in the corner of the stone terrace and sat down. Music continued to filter out the French doors and into the night air. On any other summer evening, the verdant garden would have been a sight that took her breath away. But tonight the willows and rhododendrons and the lilacs and roses blurred before her tear-filled eyes until they disappeared, like the sweet scent of the honeysuckle that was evaporating into the night air.

Luke slid onto the bench beside her.

"Why didn't you tell me you were leaving?" she asked, breaking the awkward silence that gathered between them.

"I was wrong not to."

"But why didn't you?" Her heart ached with the realization of how much she'd come to care for him. "Wait — you don't owe me an explanation. You never said or did anything to state your feelings."

He moved toward her, allowing the glow from the gas lighting to illuminate his face. She wanted to reach out and smooth a lock of his dark hair away from his forehead. To trace the curve of his strong jawline. But those were intimate things she would never do.

"I wanted to tell you how I feel," Luke began. "Every time I saw you at the shop or at the house, I had to stop myself from coming to you and asking you to wait for my return."

Rebecca stared at her hands. "Why didn't you?"

"It wouldn't have been fair to you. I won't be a man who leaves his family behind for years at a time. And besides that, I know how you feel about sailors."

Catching the sadness reflected in his eyes, she raised her brow in question. "What do you mean?"

"Do you remember when I walked you back to the shop shortly after we met? You told me —"

"That I'd never live that way." She nodded at the memory. "I could never wait year after year for the one I love to return."

That's why he'd left her so abruptly that day in front of the shop. He'd known she would never agree to wait for him. Tonight the words seemed harsh and insensitive. Nevertheless, they still rang true. She'd never have the courage to wait, wondering if he'd return to her or if the sea had swallowed him into its depth. No, living like that would be far too painful. It was better to put a stop to anything that might have started between them right now.

He caught her gaze. "Do you ever wonder what God's will is for your life?"

His question surprised her. Pulling off the velvety rose petals one at a time, she pondered the issue. Hadn't she asked God the same thing dozens of times? "It seems to be a constant question of mine lately. I want to follow His will, but more often than not I can't seem to see clearly what His will for my life is."

"Then maybe you can understand how I feel." His eyes seemed to plead with her. "I've spent my life trying to follow God's will, but more often than not I find myself pursuing the plans laid out by my parents. My father was the captain of a ship, and now my mother expects me to take the same path. Money might not be an issue, but following in my father's footsteps has always been of first importance to her."

"What do you want?"

"To work with my hands building ships."

Rebecca let the last petal fall to the ground. Building ships would mean he would no longer have to spend years at a time away from home. Instead of being a career officer at sea, he'd have time for a wife and a family. . . .

"What about this upcoming voyage?"

"I'm committed to this last trip, but after that I won't go back to sea. My mother will have to understand that I'm not my father, and what was a proper occupation for his life's work isn't the right choice for me."

A couple waltzed out onto the terrace, the woman's blue satin dress flowing in the gentle wind. They looked content and carefree as they laughed about something together. Rebecca had grown up believing God's will for her was to marry and raise a family. If that were true, then why had God put Luke in her life only to lose him so quickly? Could it be that God's will was bigger than she'd imagined?

"What if God's will is simply to live completely for Him wherever we are?" She pondered the implications of her own question. "Following Him in whatever situation we find ourselves?"

"Like your work with the orphanage?"

She nodded. "Exactly. In helping to get the quilts made for the orphans, I feel as though I'm serving God with my talents, and for the first time in a long time, I feel a deep satisfaction in what I'm doing."

Luke studied Rebecca's face in the amber light. He heard the passion in her voice and saw the obvious joy she felt in what she was doing. It was easy for him to see why he'd fallen in love with her. The difficult part was in knowing he shouldn't have.

"What about when God gives you more than one choice?" he asked. "But you can't have both." *Like the woman I love and the job I'm obligated to finish.*

"Two choices don't necessarily mean one has to be wrong. But when they conflict with each other . . ." Her smile faded.

There were no easy answers. He could speak to Captain Taft and tell him he wasn't going. Many a sailor had backed out at the last minute, knowing the hardships ahead of them. Life on a whaling vessel was grueling. Not only was the pay for the crew minimal; a good fourth of them would never make it home because of death or desertion. But no matter what was ahead, he always strove to be a man of his word. A man whose word could be counted as an unqualified guarantee. And Captain Taft was counting on him to be his first mate on the upcoming voyage.

He sat up straight and tried to loosen the tense muscles in his back. Surely God's will didn't include his losing the woman he loved merely because he'd given his word to someone else? There had to be another way. Three years would seem like an eternity, knowing he'd lost her. She'd go back to Cranton and find someone else to marry who would give her a home and a family.

The thought was sobering. Would he regret it if he never asked her if she would wait for him? Surely he had nothing to lose.

"Rebecca, I —"

"Please don't ask me to wait for you." She laid her gloved hand gently on his arm, and he flinched at her touch.

He'd known she couldn't make that kind of promise, and he wouldn't ask it of her. "Just know that if the circumstances had been different or if the timing of things would have been different —"

"I know."

He watched as she stood to leave and caught the glisten of tears against her dark lashes. What a fool he had been. He'd never meant to hurt her. If only he'd kept silent, then maybe the pain of his leaving would have been lessened. Without knowing how he felt, surely she would have quickly forgotten him.

"I'm sorry, Rebecca."

"So am I."

His hands balled into tight fists at his sides. Was it really God's will for him to lose her forever? With one last fleeting look, she hurried into the house — and out of his life.

SEVEN

It had been only three days, and Luke already missed Rebecca. He missed her bright smile and their stimulating conversations. Missed the sparkle in her eyes when she looked at him. She'd cared for him, and in turn he'd broken her heart. If only he could make her understand that he'd never intended to hurt her. That he'd never intended to come to care for her. But he did care for her, and now he was faced with the knowledge that he'd lost her forever.

Still, he wanted to see her, even if it was only for one last time. But was it worth the pain it would inflict on both of them? He knew the wisest thing for him to do was to set sail on that whaling vessel without ever seeing her again.

His shoes clicked against the hardwood floors as he strode down the hallway of his mother's home. The overcast sky created morning shadows that merged into the cream-colored walls, causing the darkened corridor to echo the gloom in his heart. Finding his mother writing letters in the parlor, he first glanced at the Baltimore clock that had characteristically stopped.

"What time is it, Mother?"

"Eight thirty," she said, glancing at the jeweled watch pinned to her dress. "I'm expecting Rebecca any minute now. She's coming with fabric samples for my bedroom. She's done such a fine job in here."

"I'm glad she's helping you, but I can't stay. I'm on my way out."

He reached down and kissed her on the cheek, wanting to escape not only a possible confrontation with Rebecca, but the constant reminders of the parlor as well. Like an artist she'd managed to brighten the room with her sense of style and color. But he barely saw the intricate details of the room. He just saw Rebecca.

"Don't forget to mail your letters," he said, turning to leave. More than once he'd found a pile of his mother's unsent letters. Attention to detail was not her forte.

"You're avoiding her." His mother dipped her pen into an ink bottle and signed her name in elegant pen strokes to the bottom of the letter she'd been writing.

"I'm not avoiding her. I'm just . . ." *Just*

what? He shook his head, realizing that in trying to avoid her, he was trying to avoid his own guilt. Nothing he could say or do, though, could take back the events that had transpired the night of his mother's party. "Could we please not talk about this right now?"

The narrowing of her eyes made him feel like a schoolboy who'd been chastised for stealing a handful of penny candy. "It was no way to treat a lady, you know. Leading her on with no intentions of furthering your relationship."

"That was never my objective, Mother, and you know it."

"Maybe not, but how do you think she views the situation?" She smoothed out the silky folds of her blue morning dress. "You visit her numerous times at the shop with an obvious hidden agenda and then bring her flowers. She couldn't help but interpret your actions as interest in her. Then without warning she finds out you're leaving, and in a most unscrupulous way, I might add."

Luke let out a long sigh. Reviewing the facts did nothing to relieve his guilt. "Then what do you propose I do? I have no doubt that at this point she wants nothing more to do with me."

"Why don't you invite her to tomorrow's

baseball game?"

"What?" Surely his mother was losing her mind. How could she, in good conscience, even suggest he do such a thing after all that had transpired between the two of them?

"We'll invite her aunt and uncle and make an enjoyable time of it."

Luke leaned his palms against the top of his mother's secretary. "And why would she agree to something like that?"

"Why wouldn't she? If nothing else, the two of you can work things out so that when you leave you won't have this vast barrier between you."

He ran his fingers across the smooth grain of the wood and shook his head. "What has come between us can't be erased with one afternoon at a ballpark. Besides, by the time I get back from the voyage, she'll more than likely be married with a couple of kids in tow."

"You don't know that. Rebecca's a fine woman, and you'd do well to mend the situation between the two of you. She has more passion and integrity than the majority of those empty-headed girls who are always chasing after you."

Luke squeezed his eyes shut for a moment, trying to grasp what his mother was implying. "Is that what you think? That I can somehow make things right between us and she'll change her mind about me? She won't wait for me, Mother. She's already made that quite clear."

"Your father and I —"

"I'm not my father." He struck his hands against the table. "Can't you see that? You expect me to live out my life the way the two of you had planned, but —"

The front door slammed shut, and he looked up to see Rebecca walk through the doorway of the parlor. His stomach churned as he drank in her beauty. She wore her hair in its normal fashion, parted in the center and secured at the nape of her neck. Her short, curly bangs framed her face and gave it a gentle softness. He had no doubt that the image of her dark brown eyes and heart-shaped face would remain etched in his memory. The same way it haunted his dreams at night.

"The housekeeper let me in. I hope you don't mind," Rebecca said.

"Not at all. I'm glad you're here." Luke's mother picked up a stack of lavender-scented sheets of paper and slipped them into the top drawer. "We were just speaking about you."

"Really?" She smiled at Mrs. Hutton but

avoided Luke's gaze. Her hesitation at seeing him at home was obvious.

"We were wondering if you, along with Ben and Clara of course, would like to spend part of tomorrow with us watching the Boston Beaneaters play."

"Oh?" Rebecca's eyes widened at the suggestion. "You like baseball, Mrs. Hutton?"

His mother's laugh was light and playful as if she didn't feel an ounce of the tension that hung between them. "Surprised that a society woman involved primarily in charity work would enjoy such a sport?"

"Well, no, but —"

"I've found it to be a pleasant distraction from time to time."

"Really?"

Confusion marked Rebecca's face, and he couldn't help but wonder if it was due to his mother's invitation or the fact that he would be there.

"Say you'll come. This will be a splendid occasion for all of us."

His heart felt as if it were about to be torn in pieces. If she agreed, it would mean that much more time he could spend with her, something he longed for desperately. But any time they spent together would make it that much harder to leave her. Could it give him a chance to make things right between them? He knew she wouldn't change her mind and wait for him. Especially after he'd foolishly waited too long to tell her the truth. But if he could be assured of her forgiveness, he wouldn't leave with the mountain of guilt that threatened to consume him.

Surely there's a way for us to be together, Lord.

Instead of a measure of reassurance for the impossible, the physical emptiness inside engulfed him like a tidal wave. The crew of a vessel always faced the threat of lost lives in the midst of a storm, but as far as he was concerned, he'd already lost his heart.

Rebecca adjusted the tilt of her wide-brimmed hat to block out the sun. She'd been surprised at the invitation and even more surprised that Luke had gone along with the request. After what he'd done to her, surely he had more sense than to think she would want to go anywhere with him. Hadn't he hurt her enough? But because it was Mrs. Hutton who'd asked, she'd agreed, not knowing how to reject the invitation politely.

Luke was obviously behind the idea, but she wasn't sure why he wanted to spend time with her. Hadn't she made it perfectly clear she had no intentions of waiting for him? Sitting on the row of bleachers that had been built for the spectators, she tried to focus on the grassy field and not the fact that Luke was sitting beside her. It wasn't as if the thought of his leaving didn't pain her. Far from it, but she knew he was someone she needed to forget. If only part of her didn't long to confess that her feelings toward him matched his own toward her.

No matter how much she wished things were different, she knew she couldn't wait for him. If he would decide to stay, they might have a chance of finding out what the future held, but she knew that would never happen either. Too much could change in three years, and they still had a great deal to learn about each other. It was better to say their good-byes and end things before it got any harder.

"This is the Beaneaters' seventy-sixth game," Luke said, turning toward her.

"Pardon?" Drawn out of her contemplation, Rebecca stole a glance at him.

"The Beaneaters," he repeated. "It's the seventy-sixth game of this year's season."

"Oh. I'm sorry. My mind must have been elsewhere."

While Aunt Clara chatted away with Mrs. Hutton and Uncle Ben dozed in the warm sun, no one seemed to notice the discomfort she felt with the situation. In fact, seating her and Luke next to each other seemed more like a matchmaking strategy.

Trying to return her focus to the events at hand, she watched as the Boston Beaneaters made their way out onto the South End Grounds. With their red stockings and padded gloves, they lined up in front of a lively crowd of spectators who stood to root for their home team. The opposing team, the Cleveland Blues, received a far less warm welcome.

"Is this your first game?" Luke asked.

"For the National League, yes."

Rebecca chewed on her bottom lip. She hated the awkwardness that had come between them. She wanted so much to forget Luke, but how could she when he sat mere inches from her?

"I assume you've watched a few of the local games in Cranton?"

"Watched? I've played dozens of those country games with my father and brothers."

"You've heard of the women's teams, haven't you, like the Philadelphia Blue Stockings?"

Playing on her father's farm after a church social was one thing. Parading around the country for the sport was another matter altogether. "I've heard that women's teams have stirred up a good bit of controversy in the past few years, even to the point that they were once labeled a dreadful demonstration of impropriety."

"And do you agree with that statement?"

At first she thought he was mocking her with his question, but with one glance she knew he wasn't. Instead he appeared genuinely interested in her opinion. And he wasn't the kind of man who would berate women and their roles in society no matter which side of the issue she stood on.

She flashed him a slight grin. "It should suffice to say that you'll never find me being paid to run around a grassy field."

As Luke chuckled in response, the Beaneaters scored another run. With Luke's attention back on the game, she let her gaze linger on his clean-shaven face. While many men wore moustaches and beards or even drooping moustaches without beards, she rather preferred the trim look. It made him look like quite the distinguished gentleman.

As the crowd settled down, he turned back to her. "May I get you something to eat from the concession stand?"

She shook her head. "I'm fine, thank you."

"Are you sure?"

"Of course." The concern on his face seemed to stem from something far weightier than wondering if she needed something to eat. "Why wouldn't I be?"

"I . . . because I never had the chance to apologize properly for what happened at my mother's party."

"You don't have to —"

"Yes, I do. Even my mother thinks I'm a cad."

In spite of the severity of his expression, she wanted to laugh at the term. He might have displayed a lack of good judgment regarding that particular situation, but he was certainly not without gentlemanly instincts. "You never acted improperly or said anything that suggested you were interested in me."

"Nevertheless, the implications were there, and I can't stand the thought of my leaving with this hanging between us."

She glanced at the rest of their party, thankful none of them appeared to be listening to their conversation. "Of course I forgive you."

Smiling, she turned back to the game. Luke Hutton was like no man she'd ever met. He certainly wasn't perfect; his omission in their conversations of his upcoming voyage was proof of that. But she could also see his strengths in the fact that he wanted desperately to make things right between them. And something told her his need for her to forgive him held no ulterior motives. He might still wish she would agree to wait for him, but even more important he wanted to do the right thing.

By the end of the game, Rebecca had all but forgotten the wall that had been erected between the two of them. She'd laughed at his commentary of the game and enjoyed his constant humor as he told her stories from his own childhood growing up in Boston.

With the final crack of the bat, the Boston Beaneaters won against the Cleveland Blues, four to zero. Watching Luke's handsome figure stand up and cheer for the home team, she was struck with the reality of their situation. Life wasn't a game of points scored, declaring winners and losers. Life, with all the joys and accomplishments one encountered, could never be measured in home runs.

Turning away from him, she knew what she had to do. If she were smart, she would protect her heart, walk away, and never see

Luke Hutton again. But what if her heart was right and he was worth waiting for?

EIGHT

Rebecca wiped away the beads of perspiration from her forehead then took the porcelain teapot out of the icebox. Earlier this morning she'd brewed a mixture of black and green tea so it would be at its peak flavor in the sultry afternoon heat. Mid-August had brought with it a number of sizzling days, and if it hadn't been for the cool breezes given off by the Atlantic, the heat would have been unbearable.

Caroline sat on the other side of the kitchen/sitting room combination of her and Philip's apartment above Macintosh Furniture and Upholstery. The pleasant room was full of detailed black walnut furnishings Philip had handcrafted, and Caroline's fabric designs gave an added cheerful feel despite the tight quarters.

While the residence was small by most people's standards, Caroline continually reminded everyone this was simply a temporary arrangement that allowed close access to the shop while their new house was being built. Despite a number of unscheduled delays, their two-story dwelling was expected to be finished before winter arrived, something Caroline seemed to anticipate almost as much as the coming baby.

"What would I do without you?" Caroline asked.

Rebecca let out a soft giggle. "You'd be suffering through this heat without the health benefits of Mrs. Lincoln's iced tea."

"All I can do is thank the good Lord that I have only five weeks left." With her feet propped up on an upholstered stool, Caroline leaned back in her Boston rocker while Rebecca finished preparing the iced tea. "Do you realize that if one has a dozen children, like Susan Parker, one is pregnant an entire nine years of her life?"

Resting her hands against her hips, Rebecca shook her head. "I do believe you have far too much time on your hands."

Caroline laughed. "Maybe, but if I don't do something, I'll go crazy. I've already told Philip that having one child will more than likely keep me plenty occupied and there is simply no reason to have another one."

"I have no doubt that once this little one comes into the world, you will completely change your mind. And as for me, someday I'd like at least three or four."

Rebecca closed her mouth and busied herself by filling the goblets full of crushed ice, wondering why she'd made that last ridiculous statement. Adding two cubes of block sugar and a slice of lemon to each glass, she tried to ignore the fact that, at the present anyway, the very possibility of children in the near future was out of the question for her. Especially since the one man she'd finally decided to take a chance with was now out of her life forever.

"Do you think I made a mistake?" Rebecca poured the chilled tea into the goblets then crossed the room to join Caroline.

"In making the tea?"

Rebecca frowned at Caroline's flippant response as she handed her one of the drinks. "Of course not. I'm talking about my decision not to wait for Luke's return."

"Honestly? I can't say I blame you."

"Really?"

Caroline took a long drink of the tea. "Too much could happen in three years, and it's not as if you have known each other for a long time. You could meet someone else, or what if he finds someone at one of the ports during the trip?"

Rebecca frowned. "Luke is not that kind

of man."

"I never meant to imply he is anything but honorable, but what about the dangers of the voyage? The life of a whaler isn't easy, whether he's the captain of the ship or the lowest crew member. The sea's never choosy about whom it decides to take."

Rebecca sat down on the end of the sofa and studied the peaceful, wintry scene of a Currier and Ives print hung on the wall across from her. The people pictured seemed to live an existence of perpetual contentment. A stark contrast to her own life. "A few weeks ago you implied it was romantic to be the lovelorn bride waiting anxiously day after day for her husband to return from sea."

Caroline ran her hands across her swollen abdomen. "As a woman close to her hour of delivery, I claim the right to change my mind on whatever subject I want, and as often as I like."

"You're absolutely incorrigible today." Rebecca shot her friend a wry grin.

"You miss him, don't you?" Caroline asked.

"I don't want to, but yes." She swirled the glass of tea in her hand and watched the ice clink against the sides. "And the sad thing is, he hasn't even left the harbor yet. He still has another few days before the ship leaves."

"You'll forget him, because life always goes on. You'll find someone who will fill the void you feel right now, and before you know it, Luke Hutton will be nothing more than a vague memory."

"You make it sound so simple." *And sad.*

"Love is never simple, but for me anyway, it helps to remember it won't hurt forever."

"I suppose you're right."

Rebecca took a sip of her tea and savored its sweetness. If only life could so easily be sprinkled with a dab of sugar to make everything work out. But as much as Caroline's words made sense, it wasn't enough. Luke wasn't just another acquaintance she could quickly forget. There was something different about him, and she wasn't convinced she'd find someone else who made her feel the way she did when she was around him.

Even what she'd felt with Jake didn't begin to compare with the deepening feelings she had toward Luke. Every time she saw him, he made her laugh, and when he was away from her, her heart felt empty. She loved the way he encouraged her to pursue her dreams for the orphanage and never made her feel she was less important because she worked as a seamstress and didn't have the wealth of so many of the girls who ran in his circles. He cared about her because of who she was, not where she came from.

Caroline leaned forward slightly. "What is it?"

Rebecca lifted her head from her contemplations. "Is my brooding that obvious?"

"I've never seen it take longer for you to drink your tea than for the ice inside the glass to melt."

Rebecca glanced down at the nearly full goblet. Today even the refreshing flavor of the tea was doing little to restore her spirits. "What if I tell him I'll wait for him?"

"You're serious about him, aren't you?"

Rebecca nodded slowly. "I don't want to lose him."

"I think you're setting yourself up for a heartache. You need to forget him. Maybe his parents did all right marrying a short time before his father left for sea, but how often do you think a situation like that works out for the good?"

Rebecca ran her finger around the rim of the glass. "I don't know."

"None of us can say what will happen between now and the time he returns. Maybe you won't have found someone else by then, and the two of you will be able to continue your relationship. Just don't close off all your options."

"I was right, you know, when I said romance with a whaler was bound to end in tragedy." Rebecca brushed back her bangs and let out a deep sigh. "Except in my situation it's a tragedy no matter what I decide to do. If I choose never to see him again, I'm afraid I'll regret my decision for the rest of my life. But on the other hand, I don't know how I could ever handle waiting so long for him to return. I'm afraid that would only bring me more heartbreak."

"I'm sorry, Rebecca. I really am. And I know none of this is easy for you. I guess all we can do at this point is pray that God shows you what to do."

"Sometimes I wonder if He cares which choice I make. He seems so far away from me lately."

"Of course He cares." Caroline set her tea on the small table beside her then leaned forward. "My mother used to quote from First Peter five, where it tells us to cast all our cares on Him, for He cares for us."

Rebecca contemplated her friend's words. "If that's true, then why does He make it so difficult to know what's best? Why is it so difficult to give up my fears and let Him take them?"

"All I can do is encourage you with the fact that He is in control and that He does love and care about you. Never lose sight of that reality."

Time was running out. With only a handful of days left until the *Liberty* departed, Luke spent the majority of his time getting both the crew and the ship ready to sail by week's end. The grueling schedule of working with Captain Taft, as well as helping Dwight Nevin put the finishing touches on the boat, gave him little time to dwell on the fact that Rebecca was forever out of his life.

Refreshed from his bath and clean change of clothes, he opened the door from his room, eager for a hot meal. Already he could smell the pungent aroma of clam chowder coming from the kitchen. Stepping into the hallway he heard the familiar sound of Rebecca's laugh coupled with his mother's.

Luke froze. His mother had told him Rebecca was coming over this afternoon, but he'd been sure she would be gone before he returned, so he hadn't worried about running into her. It wasn't that he didn't want to see her again. Not at all. But he had the memory of seeing her for the last time at the ballgame etched in his memory, and he didn't want to take the chance of spoiling it.

She'd worn a sunny yellow dress that brought out the flecks of gold in her eyes, along with a fashionable hat that had been tilted slightly to the side, giving her an elegant look. After the first few awkward minutes of watching the Boston Beaneaters play, they'd relaxed until even he had almost forgotten he was leaving.

After the baseball game they'd had no opportunity for any private good-byes between them, but he'd known that was best. He didn't want a drawn-out scene that would only bring both of them heartache. Still, he'd wanted to kiss her, to hold her in his arms and hear her say she'd wait for him; but since that could never happen, that was the way he wanted to remember their final moments together.

Knowing he shouldn't see her again, he decided to step back into his room and wait until she left; but before he could shut the door, the laughter increased, and Rebecca and his mother emerged from the bedroom.

"Luke, I didn't realize you were home. You simply must come see what Rebecca has done with my bedroom. She's just finished the slipcovers, and they look absolutely divine. They're the most stunning navy-blue and cream combination. . . ."

He barely heard his mother. All he could see was Rebecca. She stood in the doorway, her gaze firmly set on him. While a slight smile rested on her lips, he didn't miss the look of sadness in the depths of her eyes. This was what he hadn't wanted — for her to be hurt any more than she'd been already.

"Rebecca, how are you?" he asked.

"I'm doing fine, thank you." Her voice sounded formal and lacked its normal passion. "Business at the shop is very good right now."

"That's wonderful."

Suddenly he knew he wanted that private good-bye he'd missed with her. Maybe it was a foolish sentiment but one he was afraid he would regret later if he didn't at least ask. "Have you ever been up on the widow's walk on the roof of the house?"

She shook her head slowly, as if she didn't understand what he was really asking.

"The view of the ocean is incredible. I'd love to show you. . . ."

"Go ahead, Rebecca," his mother encouraged. "We're finished for the day."

Rebecca turned back to him, and he tried to read the expression on her face. Longing yet hesitation. Anticipation mixed with grief? He'd been foolish to speak so hastily.

"I'm sorry," he began. "If you need to leave —"

"No, it's fine. I'd like to see it."

As he made his way up the narrow staircase to the roof, Rebecca followed slightly behind him. He could feel the awkwardness growing between them. It was as obvious as the sound of her skirts swishing against the stone walls and the rickety steps beneath his feet. No longer could they ignore his imminent departure.

Once they were at the top of the house, he led her to the railing that secured the edge of the small widow's walk.

"The view is breathtaking." She brushed a number of loose wisps away from her face then took a deep breath of the sea air.

"This was always my favorite place to come when I was a boy."

A brisk wind blew in from the ocean, which from this point one could see for miles. An endless movement of blues and grays that met the cloudless sky in the distance. The shoreline spread out beneath them, like one of John Banvard's famous panoramic paintings that made it possible for viewers to see the world in colored detail. Waterfront businesses lined the harbor, the tide lapped against the coast, and in the distance the American flag flew proudly at the bow of a yacht.

"My father once told me about the widows' walks where the sailors' wives could come watch for the ships of their husbands to come into the harbor." Her fingers grasped the railing.

"I remember finding my mother here countless times as she watched for the *Annabella* that was to carry my father home on that last voyage."

She turned toward him. "It must have been hard for her, raising you alone for all those years he was out at sea; yet it seems to me she was content with life."

"It was always a happy life. For years my grandparents lived with us. My grandfather had acquired a sizable fortune by owning his own vessel in a time when whale cadavers were at a premium."

"Where is the *Annabella* now?"

"My father was her captain until she went down in a horrible storm off the coast of Nantucket Island."

"Is that when he died?"

Luke nodded. "A handful of men were able to make it to shore, but he went down with the ship. It was a horrible loss of life."

"I'm sorry."

"I miss that I wasn't able to know him

125

really. He died when I was quite young."

Just as he'd never understood as a child why God took his father, he didn't understand today why God had brought Rebecca into his life only for him to lose her. But if nothing else, he would try to be thankful for the times they'd shared. It would have to be enough.

"I'm thinking about going home for Christmas," she said, seeming to try to fill the silence that hung between them.

"Do you plan to return to Boston?"

"I don't know. We just received a letter, and my stepmother, Michaela, is expecting a baby sometime in January. I'd like to be home to help. And then there's my brother Adam's maple farm. They'll be harvesting the syrup early next year."

"What about your work here?"

She shrugged, and he hated the sense of despondency that had come over her. "I've already begun training a well-qualified seamstress to help with the workload. I don't think it would take much to find a second person if I decided not to come back."

"My mother will miss you." His words were foolish, and he knew it. Why couldn't he come out and say exactly what was on his heart? "I'm going to miss you."

"I'll miss you, too."

He watched her as she stared out across the ocean, and for the first time he understood why she couldn't wait for him. He'd seen his own pain mirrored in her eyes as he spoke about the loss of his father. She feared the same fate would happen to her. It had been wrong of him to hope she might agree to wait until he returned. She was young and had her whole life ahead of her. Standing on the widow's walk waiting for him was a place where she should never be.

She shivered beside him. As much as he longed to extend their time together, he knew he couldn't.

"Why don't we go back down to the house now? Once the sun drops, the temperature will fall, as well."

She looked up into his eyes, her lips parted slightly. He couldn't think. He couldn't process the reality that this was more than likely the last time he'd ever see her.

"May I kiss you good-bye?" He spoke the words without thinking, but even as he asked the question, he didn't regret it.

Nodding, she took a small step toward him. He gathered her into his arms with a passion he'd never felt before. When his lips met hers, the regret over his leaving intensified, until he lost himself in the softness of her kiss.

With tears in her eyes, she pulled away to look up at him one last time then turned toward the steps and was gone.

NINE

Trying to concentrate on the final seam of the colorful quilt top, Rebecca pushed the needle into the cream-colored fabric and winced as the sharp end jabbed her index finger. A tiny pool of blood soaked through the center of the material, ruining the square.

She let out a sigh of frustration then carefully ripped off the spoiled square. While it wasn't yet her usual hour to retire for the evening, she knew she needed to stop. The sun that had filtered light into her bedroom for the past two hours had now slipped below the horizon, so she turned up the wick slightly on the kerosene lamp. For a week she'd thrown herself into her work. During the day she ran the shop's showroom and worked on slipcover orders. By night she sewed diligently to transform the boxes of scraps into colorful quilt tops that would grace the beds of the orphans this winter.

With the involvement of Mrs. Hutton, as well as a half dozen other women from church, they'd already managed to complete five quilts for the children, leaving another fifteen to make. With the cold-weather months upon them, they couldn't afford to fall behind on the project. If only she wasn't so tired.

Yawning, she folded the quilt top then set it on the small table beside her bed. Agnes had been thrilled to hear about the upcoming donations for the children in her care, but despite the excitement she felt about the project, Rebecca still couldn't shake the restlessness inside.

Staying busy wasn't helping at all. By next week her work for Mrs. Hutton would be complete, but she had plenty of other orders that needed to be finished. Still, it seemed that as much as she tried to stay occupied, she couldn't erase the image in her mind of her last moments with Luke.

As they'd stood at the edge of the widow's walk facing the ocean, she'd been sure he was going to ask her one last time to wait for him. And at that moment, despite her earlier hesitations, she would have said yes. But instead he pulled her into his arms and kissed her, proving to her how much she was losing. When she pulled away and looked into his eyes, she knew he wasn't going to ask her to wait.

He'd only been thinking of her, and he'd been right in his decision. But being right didn't fill the emptiness in her heart. Not marrying Jake had been her decision. In the end she'd faced the situation head-on, knowing that what she was doing was best despite the fact it had been painful to let him go. With Luke things were different. It had never been her choice to end things between them, especially when she'd decided to open her heart again and take a chance on finding love.

Rebecca shoved back the chair she'd been working in then walked to the open window. Outside the moon shone brightly in the darkening sky, competing with the hundreds of stars that were making their nightly appearance. A cricket chirped below her. A dog howled in the distance. The *clip-clop* patter of a horse's hooves kept time with the lively piano tune coming from the neighbor's home. Normally she enjoyed the nightly symphony of music that played out between nature and the bustling city around her, but tonight her eyes were focused on the darkened waters of the Atlantic.

Through a small clearing in the skyline, she could see the silhouette of a boat entering the harbor. A fisherman coming home to his family after a day's work, or maybe a rich businessman returning in his yacht from a relaxing day at sea.

Luke had left three days ago. That afternoon she'd watched the tips of a ship's white sails flutter in the breeze from this window and wondered if it was the *Liberty*, the very vessel that was taking him away from her.

Her fists gripped tightly at her sides, she felt the wetness of a tear travel down her cheek. *It isn't fair, Lord. Why should I finally decide to give my heart away only to have it shatter into a million tiny pieces?*

Except for the rumbling of thunder in the distance and the normal nightly sounds, silence greeted her instead of the reply she longed for. It wasn't as if she expected God to appear before her and give her the answers, but she needed something. Some obvious sign that letting go of Luke had been God's will.

Her Bible lay on the bedside table, and she plopped onto the feather mattress and picked it up. Where was the verse Caroline had mentioned to her last week? Flipping through her Bible, she finally found the fifth chapter of First Peter. "Casting all your care upon him; for he careth for you."

She closed her Bible and hugged the book to her chest. Cast all your cares on Him. Why was it so easy to know the truth of a matter and so difficult to take it to heart? She knew God cared about her. Hadn't He created her? She knew He loved her to the point where He knew how many hairs were on her head and even counted the steps she took. Her father had made sure she knew these truths from a young age. That the God they served was not one who lived far from them but had given His Holy Spirit to live within those who followed Him.

Lord, help me to give up my fears and frustrations and learn how to follow You with all my heart. I want to find contentment in You.

Walking back to the windowsill, she watched the display of lightning brighten the distant sky. Billowing clouds had covered up all but a sliver of the moon as a storm blew in across the water. Somewhere, out among the crashing waves and endless miles of expanse, Luke was more than likely studying this very sky. How many ships now lay at the bottom of the sea from the spectacular handiwork being displayed tonight?

She pushed back a loose wisp of hair from across her face and shuddered at the thought. All she could do now was pray.

The air in the captain's cabin hung heavily around Luke. Sunlight shone through the small window, but with the dark storm clouds rolling in, the last rays of light would soon disappear. Captain Taft sat at his desk across from Luke, his elbows resting against the solid oak desk that separated them. A matter of discipline had presented itself in the early stages of the voyage. An unschooled sailor thought his philosophies of running the ship were superior to the captain's. After a fight that ended with the same young chap getting his nose split down the middle, the man had attempted to throw one of his fellow crewmen off the bow of the ship. The captain quickly took over the situation and sent the man to the brig for a couple of days of solitude. While the captain was a just and honorable man, he ran his ship with a firm hand, something Luke knew was essential for the survival of the crew.

The ship rocked beneath them, and the captain's pen rolled across the table. Lightning cracked in the distance like a whip, flashing its brilliance against the cabin walls.

"The storm's increasing in velocity," the captain said, picking up his pen and setting it into the top drawer of his desk. "This will be a good first test of how the crew works together."

Luke nodded then let out a knowing chuckle. "I'm thankful most are experienced, with the exception of our brig occupant, Mr. Lawrence. This will no doubt be a test of strength for him."

The captain rubbed his graying beard then leaned back in his chair before catching Luke's gaze. "This is going to be your last voyage, isn't it?"

Luke raised his brow in surprise at his superior's question. "To be honest, sir, the lure of the sea has never lessened for me, but I find it hard to imagine myself spending the rest of my life at her mercies. It's my parents' dream to see me captain of my own vessel, not mine."

"Then you hide your emotions well."

"Maybe, but no matter what my decision about future voyages might be, I assure you my commitment to this voyage, this crew, and to you as my captain has not diminished in the least. Nor will it until we step back on land at the end of our journey."

"I never thought it would." There was a twinkle in the older man's eyes. "Who is she?"

Luke leaned forward. "I beg your pardon?"

"Who is she? Only one thing can snatch a man from the lure of the sea — a woman."

Sensing the amusement in his voice, Luke relaxed. "There was someone, but she's not the reason for my reevaluating my future."

"Are you sure?"

"Yes, sir. My mind was pretty well made up before I met her, though I will admit she's going to be hard to forget."

"Hasn't she agreed to wait for you?"

"No, sir." Speaking the word aloud caused Luke's heart to plummet. "I couldn't ask that of her."

"Then I suggest you forget her." The captain slapped his hands against the desk. "We have a voyage ahead of us such that if our focus isn't one hundred percent on the job at hand, we'll all suffer. Lives are at stake, something I know you realize, but I know the effects women can have on my men. Unfortunately, none of us is immune to their charms at all times."

"Yes, sir. I won't forget."

After a couple of more suggestions from the captain regarding the crew's schedule, Luke made his way up onto the deck, where the winds continued to pick up. It was time to forget about Rebecca Johnson. Time to forget her captivating smile and her laugh. Besides, the captain was right. He knew if they didn't find a way to stay on the outskirts of the storm, they were in for trouble. And even if they did manage to miss the worst of the torrent, he had no doubt this was going to be a long night.

By the next morning, instead of the storm abating, it had increased in its fury. The head winds had grown stronger, and visibility was limited as the ship fought against the unseasonably strong winds. The ship's compass had been affected by the relentlessness of the storm, a serious fact considering celestial navigation was impossible because of the heavy cloud cover. Hour after hour found the crew attempting to avoid the brunt of the storm that raged around them. Luke struggled at the wheel, every muscle in his body exhausted from fighting against the winds.

The captain was worried. Luke had noticed the tension in his jaw when he'd left the bridge to supervise the rest of the crew in their endeavors to keep the ship afloat. Pounding waves continued to lash against the sides of the ship, flooding the deck with several inches of water. Luke had read plenty of accounts of shipwreck disasters and had imagined the horror of taking one's last breath of air before being swallowed into the depths of the sea. He had no desire to die that way. It had always been a reality he chose not to consider. But today things were different. It was a possibility he couldn't ignore.

Water dripped down his forehead and onto his clothes, which were already soaked from the constant barrage of waves hitting the ship. Shivering, he wiped the back of his hand across his mouth. The cup of luke-warm coffee he'd inhaled earlier had been his only source of nourishment all morning, if it could even be considered that. His stomach grumbled in complaint, but he couldn't give in to the strong desire to escape to the galley for a meal. That would come later. If it came at all.

A sharp crack ripped through the morning air as if the helm of the ship were being split in two. The vessel shuddered beneath him as it struck something. Men shouted above the commotion as they fought to save the ship. Moments later Luke saw the bright lights of a red flare being shot into the murky sky . . . then nothing.

TEN

"She's so beautiful." Rebecca sat down on the featherbed beside Caroline and ran the back of her thumb across the soft cheek of the newborn who lay nestled peacefully in her mother's arms. "I'd forgotten how small babies are."

"She is tiny, but thank the Lord she's healthy despite her early arrival." Caroline's face beamed with happiness, all the complaints of her condition forgotten with the arrival of the baby. "What smells so wonderful?"

"Hungry?"

"Famished, actually."

"Good, because I made you a thick beef stew."

Caroline's brow narrowed. "And wherever did you find the time to cook something for me?"

"Somewhere between Mrs. Kendall's

slipcovers and Myra Potter's lined draperies."

"And don't forget the quilts for the orphans. I know you've spent hours of your own time on that project." Caroline reached down and kissed the baby gently on the forehead. "You know I'm going to be spoiled before long. Susan Parker came by last night and told me several women at church would be bringing meals for the next few days. I don't think I've ever eaten so well."

"Then I won't even mention the mince pie Aunt Clara made for dessert."

Caroline groaned, but the delight was obvious in her eyes. "I just can't get over the miracle of this little one's entrance into the world."

"So," Rebecca probed, "you've decided not to stop at only one?"

"Despite a long and strenuous labor, I can't believe how in love I am with her. I don't know if three or four will be enough to satisfy my longings of motherhood."

"So Susan's twelve doesn't sound so bad after all?"

"I wouldn't go quite that far."

Rebecca laughed but couldn't ignore the stirrings she felt inside.

"Do you want to hold her?" Caroline asked.

Nodding, Rebecca gently took the baby then went to sit on the cushioned rocker that had been moved into the bedroom from the living area. The small bundle of pink whimpered softly in her arms and opened her eyes briefly. After a moment she was sleeping peacefully again.

"Have you and Philip decided on a name?" Rebecca looked up at Caroline, who still had her gaze fixed on her daughter. "It's been two days, you know."

Caroline shook her head. "The problem is that Philip has the most atrocious tastes when it comes to names. The only thing we've agreed on so far have been boy names. Of course, that was after I convinced him we couldn't name a child Milborough or Perine — family name or not."

Rebecca chuckled over Philip's awful tastes. "I would have to feel sorry for your child if given one of those names."

Caroline nodded in agreement. "The problem is, now that the Lord has blessed us with a daughter, we can't seem to come up with anything that suits us both. His first choice is Bertha after his mother. I told him that while I'm sure his mother was a wonderful woman, I have no intentions of giving my darling baby a name that sounds more like the name of a whaling vessel than a little girl."

Rebecca's smile vanished at the reminder of Luke, and she lowered her head so Caroline couldn't see her fallen expression. Reminders of him were everywhere. From the sea itself to the bouquets of flowers the street vendors sold. She'd spent half the night praying God would help her forget him, but if anything her feelings toward him had strengthened.

Rebecca took her gaze off the baby and glanced at Caroline. She was thankful her friend seemed so wrapped up in her new daughter that she didn't appear to notice Rebecca's sullen mood. She pasted on a grin. "What name had you chosen if it was a boy?"

"John. Plain yet strong. For some reason that wasn't nearly as difficult, but names for a girl . . ."

"What about Johnna for a girl?"

"Johnna." Caroline reached over and grasped the baby's hand between her fingers and smiled. "I like that name. I'll have to see what Philip thinks once he comes up from the shop for lunch. Have you thought any more about your plans for leaving?"

Rebecca glanced down at the infant, who had inherited her mother's fair skin and plump cheeks. "I think it's best for me to go home, but not until right before Christmas. That will give me a chance to help you with the baby and make sure there are competent staff to continue making the slipcovers until you're ready to take over things again."

"I'm certainly going to miss you. Michaela did well in marrying your father and bringing you into her family."

"Don't think you've gotten rid of me forever," Rebecca said, trying to lighten the somber mood that had fallen over her. "I'll have to come back and visit the baby, as well as see my grandmother someday."

"When is she due back?"

"Unfortunately, Mrs. Hutton informed me last week that she's postponed her return until late spring at the earliest."

"Well, I for one don't know what I'm going to do without you. I've enjoyed having you here."

Rebecca felt a stream of guilt course through her. "You understand why I'm leaving, don't you?"

"Of course I understand. I just hope you're not leaving Boston to escape memories of Luke."

Rebecca cringed at the statement but knew Caroline's words held a hint of truth. If only forgetting Luke was as easy to do as loving him had been.

Rebecca set the feather cushion onto the coverlet and sighed with relief. The satin, with its floral needlework pattern and lace trim, was the finishing touch in Mrs. Hutton's bedroom. Rebecca had carried the dark-blue and cream theme throughout the room, including floor-to-ceiling draperies with tiebacks and accents in the padded ottoman and throw pillows on the sofa. The overall effect was simple but stylish.

While she had no doubt she would see more of Mrs. Hutton in the coming weeks before her departure, since they worked together on the orphans' quilting project, today was the day she planned to say goodbye forever to Luke in her mind. No more would she be obliged to visit the Hutton home to measure the length of a divan or panels that would hang gracefully from cornices. No more would she have to be surrounded by the constant reminders of him that filled the house.

"Rebecca, I'm glad you're still here." Mrs. Hutton stood in the doorway, her hands clasped behind her back. "I wanted to catch you before you left."

"Is everything satisfactory?"

"Of course," she said, stepping into the

144

room. "You've done a splendid job. I wanted to make sure I had the chance to thank you again. I'm so pleased with the way the room turned out."

Rebecca smiled with relief. "I'm glad. I've enjoyed the time I've been able to work here."

Mrs. Hutton smoothed back the same strand of silver hair that seemed to fall habitually from the neat pile atop her head. But even that didn't take away from her beauty. It always amazed Rebecca to see how elegant the woman appeared no matter what the occasion.

"Mrs. Hutton, I was wondering . . ." Rebecca paused. She wanted to do one last thing before leaving the house.

"What is it, Rebecca?"

"Would you mind if I went up on the widow's walk? The view is so beautiful. I'd like to see it one last time." *And I need to say good-bye one last time.*

"Certainly, but are you all right? You seem a bit pale today."

"I'm fine. I just —" What should she say? Would Mrs. Hutton understand the feelings Rebecca felt so strongly for her son? Would she understand why she couldn't love him?

"You miss him, don't you?" Mrs. Hutton drew Rebecca onto the narrow settee that lined a section of the bedroom wall.

Rebecca nodded, determined not to shed a single teardrop. "I wish the circumstances had been different. That we'd had more time together before he left."

"And I wouldn't have minded having you for a daughter-in-law." Mrs. Hutton smiled. "I told Luke more than once that you were a good catch for a sailor like him, unlike those empty-headed girls always chasing after him."

Rebecca felt the heat rise in her face at the admission. She looked up at the wall covered with framed daguerreotypes of Luke's parents, grandparents, and other relatives. At one time she'd foolishly dared to imagine her and Luke's wedding photo gracing this very wall.

Mrs. Hutton took Rebecca's hand and squeezed it gently. "Letting go of love is never easy, even if it's the best thing."

"But was it the best thing?"

"I don't know, but I can tell you this. Right now you need to lean on God's strength. Allow His Spirit to work through you and use this situation to make you more like Him. In sixty years I've learned that life isn't always easy, but it's the experiences that have been the most painful that have taught me the most. They gave me perseverance and in the end have strengthened my faith."

Rebecca laced her fingers together, pondering the advice. "That's what I want, but instead of growing in my faith, I seem to be at a standstill. I can't hear God's voice anymore. I don't feel His presence. I'm like a raft being swept along by the tide with no real direction."

"Sometimes we can find God only in the quiet. Go on up to the widow's walk where you can see the power of His creation and just listen for His voice."

Rebecca took the narrow staircase slowly, running her hand across the cool stone walls. At the top of the house, the endless sea spread out before her. A crisp wind whipped around her face, bringing with it the signs of the coming winter. Leaning against the railing, she watched wave after wave make its way toward the shore. The ocean churned before her, and she couldn't help but wonder how Luke was faring today. But she wasn't here to daydream about him.

Instead she closed her eyes and, one by one, began erasing the memories of the two of them together. The first day they met at Macintosh Furniture and Upholstery. Their walk along the boardwalk. The bouquet of flowers he brought her. The night he told her he cared for her. The baseball game. And then the last time she saw him. Wiping her mouth with the back of her hand, she attempted to wipe away the burning memory of his kiss.

She opened her eyes again and watched as a large schooner made its way into the port. Women would be standing on their own widows' walks right now, waiting for the men they loved to return to them. Children waiting to see a father they barely remembered. Mothers ready to embrace the boy who had become a man.

But not her.

She wouldn't be here waiting when Luke returned from the sea. She wouldn't be here to welcome him home with her kisses and words of love. Instead she'd be in Cranton where she belonged, surrounded by her brothers and sisters and parents who loved her. And maybe someday she'd find a man who loved her unconditionally and whom she could love the same. Someone who shared her beliefs and passions. Someone she could grow old with.

Rebecca gripped the edge of the railing, knowing only One would never let her down.

Help me give my burdens totally to You, Lord. To let You be my strength in my weak-

ness. Help me find You again.

She'd spent her entire life trying to be strong and handle things herself. From the time she was thirteen years old, when her own mother had died, she'd been thrust into running much of her father's household. Not that she'd ever complained. It came naturally for her to care for her younger siblings, and despite the ache she'd carried in her heart from her mother's death, she'd blossomed with the responsibility.

But it had always been her own strength she'd relied on. Even with Jake she'd made the decision to call things off and move to Boston. Had she spent her life confusing her own will with God's will?

Rebecca closed her eyes again, but this time she worked to quiet her mind and focus on God and His power. To understand God's will for her life, she needed to know God. Of course she knew He cared for her, loved her, and wanted her to follow Him, but did she grasp the significance of who He was in her life? Not just her Savior, but her Lord and Master? She'd been so busy doing things that would please God, like the quilting project, but she'd devoted little time to getting to know her heavenly Father.

And it was time to change all of that.

Opening her eyes, a wave of peace washed over her. She'd taken the first step.

"Rebecca?"

Turning around, she saw Mrs. Hutton standing at the top of the staircase. Her normally calm presence had vanished, and her face had paled to the color of ashes.

"What is it?" Rebecca asked.

Mrs. Hutton leaned against the door frame. "A courier's just arrived. The *Liberty* was caught in a storm and is lost at sea."

ELEVEN

Rebecca's hands covered her mouth as she tried to grasp the news regarding the *Liberty.* She'd listened to the storms that had riveted the coastline and watched the lightning rip through the sky the past few days. Through it all she'd prayed that God's hand would protect Luke and his crew. But the *Liberty* had gone down. Surely it wasn't true. Surely this was some kind of mistake. The reality of the situation gripped her like the dark shadows of a nightmare. They'd been gone long enough that the chances of surviving that far out on the sea were too slim to expect any survivors.

The cold wind whipped around her, and she could hardly breathe. In spite of knowing it was over between her and Luke, she'd still held on to a sliver of hope that one day she'd see him again. Now every thread of hope was broken. Closing her eyes, she could see him standing beside her as he'd done the afternoon they gazed out across the sea together. She could feel his lips on hers as he kissed her good-bye. A part of her had dared to dream he would come back for her. Now she'd never know what might have happened between them.

Her eyes filled with tears. As she looked across the choppy waters, the emptiness in her heart swelled. *I miss you so much, Luke, and I'll never be able to tell you . . .*

Rebecca felt Mrs. Hutton's fingers grasp her arm, drawing her back into the present. The older woman opened her mouth, but no words came out.

"What is it?" Rebecca's heart pounded in her throat. "Is there news about Luke from the survivors?"

Mrs. Hutton nodded slowly, her breaths coming in short spurts. Rebecca didn't want to know the details of how he had died. Surely being swept into the ocean had been terrifying beyond imagination. If he'd been injured and had suffered during his last moments alive, she'd rather not know.

"Luke was —" Mrs. Hutton's fingers grew tighter around her arm. "He was rescued by another vessel."

"What?" Rebecca's eyes widened at the life preserver of hope Mrs. Hutton had thrown her.

"He's injured but alive. I've arranged for him to be brought here to the house immediately."

Tears of relief flooded down Rebecca's cheeks as she clung to Mrs. Hutton. Luke was alive! After a moment Rebecca pulled away, her ears still ringing from the news. He might be alive, but how badly was he injured? Surely God wouldn't save him from the sea only to take him from them now.

"Has he seen a doctor?" Rebecca asked.

"Only aboard the ship that rescued him. I've sent someone to go and get Dr. Neil, who is an old family friend."

Rebecca blinked, not knowing what to think. If he was alive, she had to see him. "What can I do to help?"

"Could you stay here for a while? I have no idea of his condition, and if it's life threatening —"

"Of course I'll stay. Please, just tell me what you need me to do."

While relieved at the older woman's response, Rebecca realized the request had nothing to do with her and her feelings for Luke. Patience Hutton was a mother awaiting the return of her injured son with no real clues yet as to his condition. She'd lost a husband to the sea and now was faced with the possibility of losing a son, as well.

■ ■ ■ ■

Rebecca sat in an oval-back chair in the upstairs hallway while Mrs. Hutton paced the tan plush carpet. It had been over an hour since Luke had been brought into the house then whisked away behind the closed door of his bedroom. Rebecca had begged God for Luke's healing while struggling to read through a number of the Psalms. For now she had no more tears to shed. Only a quiet desperation that filled every corner of her heart. He might have been rescued from the sinking ship, but whether he would survive the night was still in question.

At half past four the doorbell rang. The housekeeper had already dealt with a number of callers, and Rebecca was certain that news regarding the sinking of the *Liberty* had spread quickly across Boston.

One of the maids appeared at the top of the stairs. "I'm sorry to bother you, Mrs. Hutton. We've thanked and sent away the other callers, but this gentleman says he's the captain of the vessel that rescued your son."

"Tell him I'll be down immediately." Mrs. Hutton clutched her hands to her chest and turned to Rebecca. "Please, come with me."

Rebecca's stomach churned as she followed Mrs. Hutton down the stairs, anxious for more details of what Luke had gone through. She'd only caught a glimpse of him, and from his colorless features it was obvious his condition was serious. Assurances that Dr. Neil was one of the best physicians in Boston did little to relieve her fears, as she was convinced that only a miracle could save Luke now. And a miracle was exactly what she was praying for.

As they entered the parlor, an older man dressed in a simple black suit stood waiting to greet them. "Mrs. Hutton? My name is Vincent Sawyer, captain of the *Marella*."

"Mr. Sawyer." Mrs. Hutton grasped the balding man's outstretched hand. "Thank you for taking the time to stop by. May I introduce Rebecca Johnson, a family friend?"

"It's a pleasure to meet you, Miss Johnson."

"Thank you." Rebecca shook the captain's hand then took a seat on the sofa, anxious over the impending news.

"Won't you please sit down, Mr. Sawyer?" Mrs. Hutton motioned to a chair for the captain before sitting down on the sofa next to Rebecca. "Am I correct in assuming you've come with news regarding my son and the loss of the *Liberty*?"

Mr. Sawyer leaned forward in the chair. "Your son is one of the fortunate few who were able to survive in the open sea."

Mrs. Hutton held a handkerchief to her lips and exhaled deeply. "Please tell me everything. What I've heard so far has been extremely vague."

"Apparently the *Liberty* sailed into the storm a couple of days ago. Details are still sketchy, but I was on my way back from England to the Boston harbor when we came across five men who were holding on for their lives on one small lifeboat."

"How long was my son out there?"

"I can't be sure of the time line, ma'am. A number of unseasonable yet vicious storms have swept through the area these past few days, and any one of them had the potential to damage a ship."

"And my son's injuries?"

Rebecca leaned forward, listening intently to the man's words. She could hardly stand the fact that Luke lay upstairs fighting for his life and there was nothing she could do.

"I'm not a medical expert, ma'am," the captain explained, "but our ship's doctor did care for him on our return. I know his leg is injured, and he's been unconscious off and on since he was first hauled aboard our ship."

"And the other men?"

"While we were able to rescue only five of the crew, I believe they will all pull through. I've just been to see Captain Taft's wife. Unfortunately, the captain didn't make it."

Mrs. Hutton stared out the window. "I lost my husband over twenty years ago. I've always feared I'd lose my son, as well."

"Then you're fortunate God chose to save your son this time."

Two hours later Rebecca stared at the bowl of vegetable soup the cook had set before her at the dining room table. Mrs. Hutton had insisted Rebecca eat something, but so far she'd been able to take only one bite. On any other occasion she would have enjoyed the simmering bouquet of nourishment, but not today. Instead it was tasteless as her stomach churned from the morning's events. The doctor's report had been far from encouraging. At some point during the storm, Luke's left leg had been crushed. It was a miracle he'd survived the open sea for any length of time. She'd overheard whispers of amputation and shivered at what that would do to Luke. He was a man who thrived on physical work. What would the loss of an extremity do to him?

Rebecca looked up as Mrs. Hutton entered the room, her face thin and pale. Fear tightened the muscles of Rebecca's stomach as she dreaded news of Luke's worsening condition.

"How is he?"

"He's still asleep," Mrs. Hutton said. "I'm worried, Rebecca."

Rebecca worked to hold back the tears, wanting to stay strong for Mrs. Hutton's sake. Inside, though, she felt anything but strong. The doctor had left an hour ago with assurances that he'd return before nightfall. For now, they could do nothing else but wait. And the waiting was excruciating.

"Why don't you have the cook get you something to eat?" Rebecca pushed back her bowl of soup. "You need to eat to keep up your strength."

"So do you." The older woman grasped the back of the mahogany armchair at the end of the oval table. "I don't think I can stomach anything to eat, but a cup of hot tea might help calm me."

"I can't eat either." Rebecca stood from the table. "Why don't you let me sit with Luke while you rest for a while? You're exhausted and won't be of any help to him if you become ill."

She expected an argument, but instead

Mrs. Hutton nodded. "You wouldn't mind?"

"Of course not. I promise to call you if he wakes up."

Rebecca headed for the doorway but stopped when Mrs. Hutton continued. "Have you ever lost anyone close to you?"

"My mother died giving birth to my sister." Rebecca leaned against the door frame, feeling the stinging pain from dredging up the old memories. "I was thirteen years old."

Mrs. Hutton pulled out a red and gold porcelain cup and saucer from inside the reed-inlaid sideboard. "Then you know how it feels to lose someone you love. Someone you can't imagine living without."

"Like your husband?"

"I still miss him." Mrs. Hutton laid the delicate pieces on the table and sat in one of the chairs. "Our marriage wasn't perfect, of course, but we did love each other deeply."

"I'm sure he was a wonderful man."

"He was, but marrying a sailor brings its own difficulties. I would never have admitted it to Isaac, but there were moments when I wanted him to leave on the next voyage and never come back. Our time apart was so difficult."

"All marriages have their own set of

adjustments, but what you went through had to be extremely hard."

Mrs. Hutton nodded slowly, not bothering to sweep back the strand of silver hair that had once again fallen out of place. "The last time I saw him before he left on the *Annabella* was early on a misty autumn morning. I was mad at him over some silly misunderstanding we'd had the night before, but at the time I was stubborn and didn't want to believe our argument was partly my fault. When he kissed me that last morning, I let him walk away without saying good-bye to him. How could I have been such a fool? I never saw him again."

The room was silent for a moment. Rebecca bowed her head and studied the intricate pattern in the Oriental rug. She'd seen the pain of past mistakes etched into the creases around the older woman's eyes, but what could she say that would make a difference?

"I've never forgiven myself for wishing he wouldn't return," Mrs. Hutton continued. "For months after his death, I blamed myself, somehow thinking God heard my grumbling and decided to teach me a lesson."

"God doesn't work that way."

"I know He doesn't, but sometimes my

heart has a hard time accepting what I know is true."

"How well I understand that." Rebecca let out a deep sigh. She had no doubt that God had never left her; yet how easy it was to feel the void of His presence when things became difficult and the answers seemed so far away.

Mrs. Hutton traced her index finger around the rim of the empty cup. "I told you earlier that life isn't always easy, but it's the painful experiences that have taught me the most. Realizing Isaac wasn't coming back after the horrid things I said to him was one of those instances that took me years to work through. I think that's why I've always encouraged Luke to follow in his father's footsteps — maybe too much — but I haven't wanted the guilt from my own past to stop him from doing what he wants to do."

"I'm so sorry you had to go through that."

"Luke's accident brings it all back to me. I'm so afraid of losing my son. You understand, don't you, because you love him?"

"Yes," Rebecca said, squeezing her eyes shut at the admission. "I love him."

Fifteen minutes later Rebecca sat in a chair at Luke's side, a weathered Bible open in front of her. But with her eyes filled with tears, she couldn't focus on the words. If she hadn't heard the doctor's diagnosis, she could almost believe Luke was simply sleeping peacefully. Instead she feared that each breath he took might be his last. And she couldn't lose him now.

Shutting the Bible, she looked around the room at signs of the boy who had turned into a man. A pupil's copy of *McGuffey's Eclectic Reader* lay beside Ralph Waldo Emerson's *Nature* and James Fenimore Cooper's *The Last of the Mohicans.* A pair of hardened steel skates sat precariously on the floor. On his desk perched a brightly painted cast-iron bank, cleverly engineered so that the little mechanical dog would leap through a clown's hoop and drop a penny in the barrel for safekeeping.

Realizing Luke was alive had made her feel as if God was giving them a second chance to find love with one another. A second chance to let go of their fears and trust in Him completely to show them what direction He would have them take. But was this truly a second chance? She tried to pray, but her words seemed empty. Mere words seemed insignificant when searching for God's will in her life — and when begging for God to save the life of the one she loved.

■ ■ ■ ■

Luke felt a piercing pain rip through his leg and struggled to open his eyes. Why did it hurt so much? A shiver swept over him, reminding him of the dark, cold waters. The ship had hit something; then he'd felt the sea pull him under. But he wouldn't let it win. He wasn't ready to die, so he'd clung to something until —

"Luke?" He could hear Rebecca's voice, but he couldn't find her. "Are you awake?"

He groaned and forced his eyes open. The room swirled around him like a dark fog. It was his room. He recognized the mechanical bank his grandfather had given him. In the distance . . . a shelf of books . . . When had he returned home?

"Luke, it's Rebecca."

He turned his head toward her voice, gritting his teeth at the intense pain that refused to leave him.

"You're home now. It's going to be all right."

Too exhausted to talk, he closed his eyes again. Despite the searing pain, only two things seemed to matter. Rebecca was with him, and he knew he loved her.

TWELVE

Rebecca set the worn copy of *The Golden Trail* in her lap and smiled across the small stretch of green lawn toward Luke's sleeping form. Six days after his rescue, he was still confined to a wheelchair; but the color in his face was back, and on most days his spirits had been high. Leaning against the rough bark of the oak tree that majestically towered above her in the Hutton garden, she let out a contented sigh of relief. Only God knew what the days ahead of them would hold, but for the first time a life spent with Luke seemed possible.

Only one dark shadow hovered in the recesses of her mind. While the doctor had decided against the necessity of amputating the injured extremity, full use of the limb was still questionable. Because of the uncertainties that lay ahead, Luke spoke little about the future, except for telling her that his days spent on a whaling voyage were over. He seemed to accept this without remorse, and she hoped his acceptance of the matter was because of her. With him now free from the obligations of the sea, they had been offered the chance to pursue a future together. Whether he still wanted to take that chance, she wasn't sure.

Luke's eyes opened halfway. "Why did you stop reading?"

"You were asleep."

"I was not."

"You were snoring." Rebecca laughed. "You know, between the cook's succulent dishes and your orneriness, you might actually recover."

Luke folded his arms across his chest and frowned. "So what did I miss?"

"In the book?"

He nodded, appearing disinterested in the story, but she knew that was far from the truth. He'd had to spend most of his time lying in bed for nearly a week, and she knew he enjoyed the hours she spent reading to him from either the Bible or the dozen dime novels she kept tucked away in her mother's wooden trunk.

She hugged the yellow-spined book to her chest. "Cassidy Walker, the wicked villain of the story, was sent to jail for robbing one of the transcontinental railroads. Max Crane, on the other hand, was heralded a hero for his daring role in saving the town's fortune of gold. And in the end, of course, the beautiful Bessie was so awed by his bravery that when he asked to take her hand in marriage, she swooned, but not before saying yes to his proposal."

Luke's gaze shot to the sky, and he shook his head at her dramatic rendition of the story's ending. "Perhaps it's time you tried a new profession. You could let your imagination run wild while teaching lessons in morality, like how being honest has its rewards."

Her eyes widened at his teasing. "You can't be serious. My dull imagination would have people closing the covers before they reached page two."

Luke laughed. "Maybe, but I still can't believe you got me to listen to one of those dime novels."

"You're bored silly, and you know it. Besides, what's so horrible about them?" She held up the book and pretended to be miffed. "Evil is punished, and virtue is well rewarded. Besides, you enjoyed every minute of this tale, didn't you?"

"Something I certainly would never admit." He winked at her. "One thing I have noticed, though, is in the end the hero always gets the fair maiden."

Rebecca sucked in her breath and held it as he looked at her. His eyes glistened like tiny fireworks as they caught the last rays of the setting sun. The dark outline of a beard covered his strong jaw. All she wanted to do was sit and watch him, hardly able to believe he was alive and with her again. But he was here, and each day she spent with him, she found herself falling deeper and deeper into his charms.

"It seems a lifetime ago that you let me kiss you on the widow's walk." His words came out huskily as he spoke of the very moment she'd dreamed about for days.

"For me, as well."

Fiddling with a blade of grass between her fingers, she stared at it and longed for him to tell her of his intentions toward her. Longed for him to take her in his arms as he had that moment when they'd over-looked the sea, knowing he was leaving. He'd captured a part of her heart the way no man ever had. And a part of her never wanted to take it back.

But one question haunted her. She'd seen the way he stared across a room or the garden when he didn't know she was watching him, his eyes full of pain and grief. It was obvious the accident had changed him.

Had it also changed things between them? Was it possible, despite his teasing, that now that he was here to stay, he regretted his impulsive actions toward her?

She twisted the thick blade until it split under the strain. She'd come to the Hutton home every day since the accident, telling herself it was simply to help Luke's mother deal with the difficult recovery. But she knew that wasn't true. She'd come because of Luke. Because she longed to see him and be near him. It was as if letting him out of her sight might mean she'd lose him again forever.

"Everything seems different now, Rebecca."

Her chin darted upward, and she cringed at his words as she waited for him to continue.

"I don't know why God let me live while most of the other men on that ship lost their lives."

"You know the accident wasn't your fault."

"I know." He shrugged his shoulders. "But I also know things will never be the same again."

"You're right." She leaned forward and rested her palms against the cool grass. "Those men's families will never see them again — children who lost their fathers, women who lost their husbands. There's an emptiness that will never be replaced. And as for your own injuries . . ."

She watched as his fingers gripped the bulky blanket on his lap. He was right. Things would never be the same again. Life might go on, but it was clear that a part of him had died when the *Liberty* went down.

"Is it crazy to want to know why God saved me and not the others? Captain Taft was a good man with a wife and three children. Williams, our cook, had a son born three months ago who will never know him." His jaw tensed, bringing out the veins in his neck. "How could God let something like this happen?"

"I don't know, Luke."

She swallowed hard, praying that God would help her to know what to say. The pain in his eyes flashed before her, his grief obvious from the tone of his voice. She couldn't even imagine the things he'd seen and heard during those fateful moments when the sea swallowed his friends and crewmates into its depths. It was a tragedy whose consequences would be felt for decades by those left behind.

"I've been struggling lately with the feeling that God is so far away and not knowing what He wants me to do with my life."

Trying to formulate her words, she stared at the last streaks of color from the sunset as they faded into the darkening skyline. "I haven't been able to feel His presence, and when tragedies like this occur, it leaves me questioning His role in my life.

"I found a verse in Hebrews that I've clung to these past few days. It tells us to hold fast the profession of our faith without wavering, because He's faithful. Life is full of difficulties, but in the end, if we persevere, we have victory through Christ and will be with Him forever in the place He's preparing for us."

" 'In the world ye shall have tribulation: but be of good cheer; for I have overcome the world.' " He shot her a half smile. "My mother used to quote that verse to me frequently."

Rebecca smiled back, despite the deep conviction the verse brought her. "It's still hard putting the words into practice, though, isn't it?"

"I definitely feel caught between what I believe to be true and knowing how to put it into practice."

"Trust me — you're not the only one."

He leaned back in the chair and looked at her. "I'm sorry to have switched to such a serious subject."

"I'm not. I, too, have so many questions regarding the matter. I guess I just have to cling to the truth that He is faithful."

"And the other subject we started talking about? The one about you and me —"

She glanced away from Luke, momentarily distracted as Philip, Caroline's husband, stepped down from the terrace and onto the lawn. "If the two of you are ready to come in, the rest of us can start eating dinner."

With her heart still pounding at Luke's last comment, she stood and managed a polite nod. What had Luke wanted to say? Had he finally planned to ask if he could court her, or had he changed his mind and wanted only to tell her the truth about his new feelings?

"You're fortunate Mrs. Hutton invited you for dinner tonight, Philip," Rebecca said with a forced laugh as she maneuvered Luke's chair toward the house. "I do believe that all you men think about is food."

Luke cleared his throat and looked back at her. "I have to confess, now that my appetite is finally back, I always seem ready to eat."

Rebecca pushed Luke to the bottom of the stairs, where Philip waited to help maneuver the chair into the dining room, wondering all the while what tomorrow might hold.

Luke felt the light breeze filter in from his open bedroom window and wheeled his chair closer so he could look out over the silhouette of a city preparing to sleep for the night. Familiar sounds of dogs barking and the occasional raised voice played against the softer sounds of the incoming waves of the nearby sea, that vast churning beast that seemed to take life as easily as it provided for it. How strange that the very sea that had taken him away from Rebecca had been the same sea that now sent him home.

He let out a deep sigh, both out of frustration and out of longing. Life seemed so full of uncertainties. Not that he doubted God's presence in his life, but that didn't change the fact that He often seemed farther away than the distant shores Luke visited on his last voyage. Still, Rebecca's words had reminded him of his Creator's constant care despite the dreadful events he'd somehow survived. But even that knowledge didn't erase the pain burning within his soul.

He didn't understand why he lived when the majority of the crew, including his captain, had perished in the accident. How could he not question the purpose of his survival? God might have a plan for his life, but at the moment, with a useless leg, he had no idea what it might be.

Like Rebecca, their minister had come by and assured him any guilt he felt over his crewmates' deaths was normal, but instead of feeling absolved, he fought against feelings of remorse. He longed to find the reason why God pulled him out of the depths of the sea. Being thankful for his survival wasn't always easy, in spite of the fact that he knew he had a lot to be grateful for. Friends, family . . . Rebecca.

He'd seen the glimmer of hope in her expression as she spoke about God's unfailing care and love and wished he could feel the peace she exhibited despite her confessed uncertainty at times.

All week her smile had given him a reason to fight. The doctor might not be sure how far his recovery would go, but with Rebecca's encouragement he'd made significant progress. His biggest hurdle now was getting out of the chair to which he was temporarily affixed. But he was determined to walk. He'd overcome numerous obstacles in the past, from a life-threatening case of measles as a child to the sun-scorched conditions on a whaling vessel. His own fortitude of mind refused to allow this newest barrier to stop him. The doctor had managed to save his leg. It was up to him to get out of the chair.

Luke stared out his window as a shooting star streaked across the blackened sky. Higher on the horizon the moon hovered like a brightly lit whale-oil lamp. He knew that the God who displayed His majesty in the heavens above as well as the earth below could bring healing to his battered body, but would He bring peace to his troubled soul, as well?

Turning away from the window, Luke edged his way toward the bed as fatigue took over his body. Philip's presence in the house tonight at dinner had affected him, as well. As Philip spoke about his wife and new daughter, Luke could vividly imagine the joy he hoped to feel one day about his own family. Isn't that what he wanted at some point? A wife, a family, and a place to call their own? And he was certain he wanted to spend that life with Rebecca. Before Philip had interrupted them in the garden, he'd planned to speak to her about his intentions. He yearned to tell her it was time they took a step forward with their relationship if she would agree to allow him to court her officially.

He gripped the arms of his chair as the reality of his situation rushed over him. Maybe it was good he'd missed the chance to say anything. Certain questions haunted not only his waking hours, but also his dreams at night. What if he was never able to walk again? How could he, as a cripple, support Rebecca? He'd always felt that God's will for him revolved around the bounty of the sea, both through his past whaling voyages and his dream of building ships. Without his legs, though, finding a purpose for his life seemed hopeless.

Parallel to the edge of his bed, Luke stifled the urge to call for the man his mother had hired to assist him. A week had already passed, and while he felt somewhat stronger, it was time to push his physical limits. He refused to rely on this chair or other people for the rest of his life.

Forcing his tired arms to push his body out of the chair, Luke felt his muscles burn with the effort, but he refused to give in to the pain. He set his good leg on the floor and stood slowly. He swayed with the effort then caught his balance. One step was all he needed to take. One step and the exertion would be over. He felt a spasm in his leg, and it refused to move.

Struggling to fill his lungs with air, he let

his other foot touch the ground. Tiny beads of perspiration broke out across his forehead. Closing his eyes, he could envision Rebecca's face before him. She would tell him to keep on no matter how much his body revolted against the effort. And that's exactly what he planned to do.

His injured leg brushed against the floor, shooting a wave of fire through the extremity. Clenching his teeth, he fought the swelling pain that surged within him and tried to regain his balance. But determination wasn't enough. With a loud groan Luke crumpled into a heap on the rug.

THIRTEEN

"You haven't heard a single word I've said, have you?" Rebecca sat back in the padded wicker chair on the Huttons' terrace and frowned at Luke's somber figure.

For the past few days, she'd managed to juggle her time between fulfilling her responsibilities at the furniture shop and staying up late into the night to complete the remaining quilts for the orphans. In addition, she'd continued to keep Luke company in the afternoons. While spending time with him was something she'd come to enjoy during his recovery, his sullen attitude these last couple of days had tempted her more than once to send her regrets that she would not be available to stop by. If he simply wanted someone to be around, the maid could do that.

Matching her frown, he said nothing as he slid his knight across the wooden chessboard.

She folded her arms across her chest. "I didn't come to sit and talk to the wall."

"Then why did you come?" He looked up, exposing the pair of atrocious muttonchops he'd allowed to grow along the sides of his face. Others might contend that such a look was fashionable, but she did not.

Rising from the table she glanced into the house, wishing Mrs. Hutton hadn't gone out. Luke's mother had assured her the daily afternoon visits lifted his spirits and had invited her to continue coming until he was walking again. It was something she'd done with pleasure. Until today.

At the moment she wasn't even sure why she had come. Not once had he made further mention of his intentions toward her, leaving her at a loss as to where their relationship, if there even was one, was headed. In fact, the conversation they'd begun the other night regarding their future had seemingly vanished along with the fading daylight.

"It's your turn." Luke's fingers gripped the armrest as he rocked his chair back and forth.

The slight squeak coming from the left wheel was enough to drive her mad, and while she hated venting her own frustrations on him, she was tired of his unpleasant moods. "I'd rather not play anymore."

"Would you prefer reading to me?"

"Reading to you?" Rebecca plopped back down in her chair, exasperated. After his long-winded complaints about the ending of the last dime novel she'd read him, she was surprised he had the gall to ask. "You want me to read to you?"

A fire blazed in his eyes as he looked at her. "Honestly? No. I don't want you to read to me. I want to go down to the harbor and start building another boat. I want to wear my ice skates and spend the afternoon at the indoor rink. I want to —"

"Luke —" She clenched her teeth together.

"What? What do you want to say? That I can't do any of those things now?" He leaned forward in his chair. "Don't you know I'm fully aware of what I can't do anymore?"

With one long brush of his hand, Luke swept the chessboard onto the stone floor of the terrace, its wooden armies scattering in every direction. The following silence was deafening. Rebecca stared at the jumbled pieces strewn across the ground and was overcome with a sense of guilt. He may have lost his temper, but she'd helped drive him to it. Who was she to judge his unpleasant attitude when he'd been through so much? On top of watching the horrendous deaths of his crewmates, he'd possibly lost not only the use of one of his extremities, but his dream to be a shipbuilder. Didn't the man have a right to go through a time of mourning?

"I'm sorry." Their apologies came at the same time, bringing a slight grin to Rebecca's lips.

Luke ran his fingers through his wavy hair. "You have nothing to regret. I'm the one who's been truly horrible these past few days. I really am sorry."

"Wanting to quit the game because I was irritated at you wasn't exactly model behavior either."

He tilted his head slightly. "Why do you keep coming every day to see me?"

"What do you mean?"

"Look at me." He lifted the blanket off his useless leg. "The doctors aren't sure I'll ever walk again on my own. I'm grumpy and more ornery by the minute. Why do you bother coming at all?"

She picked up one of the chess pieces that had fallen into her lap and rolled it between her fingers. Why did she continue to come, day after day? Why did she put up with his cantankerous attitude and his impossible disposition? It wasn't as if she had to come. She had no claims on him.

You've come every day because you still love him, Rebecca Ann Johnson.

Rebecca swallowed hard at the confession. As afraid as she was to love him, it was an emotion she couldn't ignore. And she realized now the question she had to ask despite the searing pain his rejection would bring.

"I need to know your intentions by me, Luke. I know the accident changed you. If you want me to walk out of your life today, then I'll never bother you again. But if what you said to me that night in the garden is still true . . . I need to know."

"I've been such a fool." He shook his head slowly then squeezed his eyes shut for a moment.

Her heart thudded as she studied his solemn expression, dreading his response. She was the one who had been the fool. He didn't love her anymore. She could see it in his face. His head dropped as he avoided her gaze. He may not want to tell her the truth, but she had to know.

Besides, she should have known that now that no excuses stood between them — no three-year voyage saving him from having to make a commitment — his true feelings would eventually surface. She'd seen what she wanted to in the situation, not the true reality of what was. Had she believed Luke Hutton cared about her when he could have any woman he wanted? Nausea washed over her. They lived in two different worlds, and she'd been childish to believe their relationship could have a happy ending like one of her cheap dime novels.

He leaned forward in his chair. "I told you the other day that everything has changed for me, but one thing I don't think ever will, and that's how I feel about you."

Her brow wrinkled in confusion. "I — I thought —"

"I still love you, Rebecca."

Any traces of anger or frustration vanished from his face. She couldn't breathe. Had he really told her he still loved her? A smile broke out across her face as the reality of his words began to sink in. Luke Hutton loved her. But as a shadow crossed his face, she knew there was more.

"What is it?"

He pressed his fingertips together before speaking. "I don't know if I'll ever be able to walk again. I might have a nice-sized inheritance from my father, but I don't know if I can survive that way. Living day after day in this chair, being forced to rely on others for everything I want to do. You deserve more than a man who's an invalid."

Tears sprang to her eyes, and she shook her head. "When you left on the *Liberty,* I thought I'd lost you forever. I was the foolish one who refused to wait for your return even though I knew I loved you. If you really love me, please don't let this get in the way of us."

Luke felt the tension grow along his jawline. His first impulse at her question had been to tell her a lie. If he told her he didn't have feelings for her, it might make it easier for her in the long run. She'd go home to Cranton and forget about the washed-out sailor who'd more than likely never navigate another ship again, let alone build one. He didn't want to be a burden to her.

But as much as he'd wanted to, he knew he had to tell her the truth. How could he deny his feelings to the one woman who had completely stolen his heart? No matter what he did, he felt trapped.

"What if I never walk again, Rebecca?"

"What if you do?" A look of determination flashed in her eyes. "It hasn't been that long since they dragged you out of the ocean, clinging to a dilapidated lifeboat. You're going to walk again someday — I know it."

He laughed aloud as all the frustrations from earlier melted away. "Now I know why you've been coming."

"And why is that?"

"To give me the swift kick of motivation I need each day. You're right for me, Rebecca Johnson. I need you in my life."

He noticed the crimson blush that crept up her ivory skin, giving her a radiant glow. A smile lingered on her lips. "Then we'll have to take things slowly so I can make sure you're going to behave."

"Yes, ma'am."

Fumbling with the pawn in her hand, she laid it on the chessboard then knelt on the ground to pick up the other escaped soldiers.

I don't deserve her, Lord. But whatever Your will is for my life, after all that's happened, she's the one thing that still makes sense.

But would she decide to stay? She was close to her family, and the desire to be with them was pulling her away from Boston. It was something he understood, but would she stay long enough for them to see if a relationship between them would work? And what about after that? Could he move to Cranton, leaving behind his mother and the sea that still called him? He seemed to have far more questions than answers.

"What about your going home to Cranton?" he asked.

"I'd still like to go and visit my family, but now I'd have a reason to return to Boston." She looked up at him. "And if you're up and walking by Christmastime . . ."

He couldn't help but hope her subtle invitation was one offered in all seriousness. Throughout the time they'd known each other, he'd enjoyed numerous stories of her six brothers and sisters, from how Samuel presented their stepmother, Michaela, with a frog the first time they met her, to how they had adopted little Anna from the Mills Street Orphanage. While he had never met any of them, he could picture them clearly in his mind. Sarah, who loved to talk almost as much as she loved her animals; Adam, who dreamed of running his own maple syrup farm . . .

All his life he'd longed for a big family, and while the thought of meeting Rebecca's relations might be a bit overwhelming, he wanted to be a part of them.

Luke watched the hem of her purple dress sweep against the stone flooring as her slender fingers scooped up the remaining pieces. He'd never noticed how her lips pressed together when she concentrated on something or how when she tilted her head she gnawed on her lip.

Trying to ignore the throbbing pain in his knee, he thought about the night the *Liberty* sank. He'd thought she was there with him. He remembered now. He'd heard her voice as he clung to the board. She told him not to give up. Not to let go of hope. Frigid waters had swirled beneath him, threatening to ravage his weakened body. He remembered the warmth of her kiss and the taste of her lips, and as he prayed for deliverance, he somehow found the strength to hold on.

Slowly he rolled the chair around the table and across the terrace. Even from where he was, he could smell the flowery scent of her perfume captured by the afternoon breezes. He moved until he was mere inches from her.

"You know you need to grease your wheel." She turned to him, her hands filled with the last of the chess pieces.

"Really? I didn't notice." How could he when she was all he noticed?

She moved to stand then stopped at the sound of ripping fabric. She let out a sharp breath. "Luke, my dress — it's caught beneath your wheel."

Unable to stop himself, he laughed aloud

but made no attempt to move the chair. "I seem to remember another time you were entangled by my charms."

"It was a rosebush," she said with a giggle, examining the front of her dress.

Resting her hands on one side of the chair, she pushed it back slowly until the garment was free. He leaned toward her until he could feel the whisper of her breath against his cheek.

"You're going to have to be more careful with this contraption." She let go of the chair but didn't move away. "You're liable to catch some poor girl in it."

"There's only one girl I have any desire to capture."

"And who would that be?"

"You."

Laughing, she tried to pull away but not before he caught her in his arms. Lightly he brushed his lips across hers before letting her go.

The sun spun a halo of gold above her. "What happens next?"

"I believe I have some hard work ahead of me." He squeezed her hands between his fingers. "If I'm ever going to court you, I have to be able to walk again."

Rebecca ambled up the brick walk toward

Aunt Clara's home, a lazy smile across her face. The two-story home loomed ahead of her with its corbeled brick exterior and arched windows, obstructed only by the giant oak trees whose yellow leaves fluttered to the ground around her. Back in Cranton, Michaela had recounted dozens of stories pertaining to her growing-up years in Boston with Aunt Clara. Fond memories of Christmases spent in front of the stone fireplace, evenings singing carols and drinking hot chocolate, and especially the fact that the house had been filled with love. In the short time Rebecca had lived here, she'd come to feel as if she'd known Aunt Clara her entire life. She was the grandmother she'd never known.

Taking the porch steps two at a time, she wondered if maybe God's will for her life had always been right in front of her. She hadn't known how much she cared for Luke until she lost him. Now that he was back, she knew she never wanted to let him go.

Aunt Clara opened the door, and Rebecca wrapped her arms around the older woman, content with the way her life had turned. After a moment she stepped back, but before she could say anything, she caught the quiver in the older woman's chin and the white pallor of her face.

"Aunt Clara? What's happened?"

Aunt Clara squeezed Rebecca's shoulders and didn't let go. "We received a telegram from your parents a short while ago."

Rebecca's hands covered her mouth. Her parents had never sent anything but letters. If something was wrong with a member of her family . . .

"Come inside, Rebecca, and sit down."

Obeying, she followed her aunt into the parlor. The normally cheery room turned gloomy. Even the pale rays of sunlight spilling across rose-colored walls couldn't brighten the impending despair she felt.

Sitting next to the older woman on the flowered slipcovers, Rebecca leaned forward. "What is it, Aunt Clara? Please tell me."

Aunt Clara gathered Rebecca's hands between her wrinkled fingers. "The telegram was brief, so we don't have all the details, but your brother Samuel was involved in a serious accident."

Rebecca worked to slow her breathing. He'd sent her a letter a few weeks ago telling her about a girl he'd met. At seventeen he might not be ready for the responsibilities of starting a family, but from his penned words he was quite smitten with the girl.

Please, God, whatever it is, let him be all right.

"What happened? How is he?"

Aunt Clara shook her head slowly. "Apparently his injuries were quite severe. I'm sorry to have to tell you this, Rebecca, but Samuel died this morning."

Fourteen

Rebecca stepped onto the stone terrace behind the Hutton home, unsure how she was going to tell Luke she had tickets for the afternoon train to Cranton. Had it been less than twenty-four hours since he'd kissed her in this very place and told her he still loved her?

I don't understand, God. Just when I thought things might work out between Luke and me . . .

He sat in a patch of sun at the edge of the terrace, reading his Bible. She watched him unobserved for a moment, unable to stop wondering how long it would be until she would see him again. In the midst of her sorrow over Samuel's death, the darkness of last night had brought with it the old seeds of doubts over God's will for her life. Surely her brother's death hadn't been a part of God's perfect will. A cloud of confusion weighed her down as she struggled to hold on to the fibers of her faith.

But despite the gnawing uncertainties that plagued her over her family's loss, she knew that whatever the future might bring, she loved Luke. She wanted him to hold her. To tell her everything would be all right. To tell her this was nothing more than a horrid nightmare and when he kissed her she'd wake up and discover it had all been a terrible mistake —

"Rebecca?" He looked up, his smile revealing how happy he was to see her. He closed the Bible in his lap and pushed the chair toward her. "I hadn't expected to see you until this afternoon."

"I needed to speak to you about something."

"Why don't you come and sit by me?" He paused for a moment and furrowed his brow. "What's wrong?"

She knew she looked dreadful. Before she left Aunt Clara's home, she'd glanced into the beveled mirror in her room. Her eyes were red from crying, and her normally rosy complexion had turned into a chalky shade of white. In her losing Samuel, one of the bright lights in her life had been snuffed out forever.

Ignoring the pain in her heart, she tried instead to focus on memorizing every detail of Luke's face before she left. His cleft chin, eyes the color of maple sugar, his broad shoulders and solid form. Her heart thudded, reacting to his nearness. He'd even shaved, ridding himself of those horrid muttonchops. She noticed another change in his countenance as well. It was as if the anger and frustrations he'd been experiencing had all but disappeared. Would what she was about to say change that?

"Rebecca, what is it?"

She clutched her hands together and sat down on the padded chair beside him, wondering where to start. How could she tell him she was going away and had no idea when she planned to come back to Boston? How could she tell him about her brother?

"Samuel's dead." She hadn't meant for it to come out so blunt — so cold. Saying it aloud made it final.

"What?" She saw a flash of pain in his eyes, a look of shock that mirrored her own feelings. He reached out and took her hand. "I'm so sorry. What happened?"

She shook her head, trying to steady her breathing. "I'm still not sure about many of the details. Samuel's always been a bit of a daredevil, but this time someone else was involved. Samuel threw the first punch and must have pushed him too far, because the other boy . . . he . . . he had a gun."

"And he shot your brother?"

Rebecca nodded, fighting back the sting of tears. "Adam was there and tried to stop it but couldn't. They don't even know the other boy's name."

She thought she'd cried until her heart was dry the night before, but she was wrong. Tears began to stream down her cheeks, bringing another measure of soul-wrenching grief. She was angry at Samuel for taking an unnecessary risk and losing his life over a stupid argument. Angry because now she'd never see him again.

Luke rubbed the backs of her hands with his fingers. She felt comfort in his touch but realized that even in his presence he could do nothing to take away the pain she was experiencing.

"He was seventeen years old," she began between sobs. "He dreamed of becoming a doctor someday. I can still remember so vividly when he and Adam spent countless lazy summers fishing along the Connecticut River. Samuel was always the first to pull pranks on the rest of us."

She smiled at the memory, wishing she could bring back those carefree days before one tragic moment had changed everything so drastically. "He used to sit in the parlor with Adam and my father, devouring copies of Orange Judd's *American Agriculturist* for information on scientific farming while planning out their own ideas on how to better develop the land. Samuel's the one who encouraged Adam to expand his maple syrup farm."

Now her brother had been killed for no reason. One malice-driven bullet had waylaid every one of Samuel's dreams.

Luke lifted her chin and turned her head toward him. "You're going home, aren't you?"

"Uncle Ben's waiting for me outside, but I couldn't go without saying good-bye to you."

Her lip quivered. She was only inches from his face. So close she could read the sadness in his eyes and see the tremor of pain in his expression. She could hardly stand being so close to him and knowing that in a few minutes she was going to walk out the door. She didn't want to make things any more difficult than they already were.

And she felt torn. Torn not only by the conflicting emotions surrounding Samuel's death, but also by the fact that she was leaving. Luke's physical recovery wasn't going to be easy, and she wanted to be here to encourage him; yet she knew she needed to be with her family, as well. If only Luke could come with her —

"Do you have any idea how long you'll be gone?" Luke asked.

She shrugged. "I don't know. With Christmas barely three months away, I thought it might be best to stay at least until after the New Year, but then Michaela's baby is due in January. And Adam is not taking this well. I'm hoping I can be there for him. We've always been close."

She stopped, not knowing how to say the remaining thoughts that lingered in her heart. Samuel's death had spun her world into a mass of confusion. She would miss her grandmother's return and Luke's recovery —

"Go home to your family." He leaned forward and wiped away her tears with his thumbs then brushed his lips across hers. "Before long I'll be walking again and waiting for you as long as it takes."

She leaned into the warmth of his arms and prayed he was right.

Rebecca shoved the heel of her hand into the smooth bread dough then flipped it onto the floured board. Returning to Cranton had been dreamlike for her. While a few new stores lined the town's wooden sidewalk, it appeared little had changed. As they'd pulled in front of the gray-shingled farm-house where she grew up, she'd been greeted by not only the familiar acres of farmland, bordered with stone fences and tall elm trees, but also the subdued welcome of her family.

Only one thing had undeniably changed. Samuel would never be with them again.

Beside her, Michaela worked on rolling out a piecrust, seeming to know instinctively that Rebecca needed the quiet. Her step-mother may not have given birth to Sam-uel, but the love she had for him was clear in her eyes. It mirrored that of her father's and the rest of Samuel's siblings. A part of all of them was gone.

"I still can't believe what happened," Rebecca said, breaking the silence between them.

"None of us can, dear."

Feeling restless, Rebecca paced to the window and looked out over the familiar landscape where summer was now giving way to autumn and its golden woodlands. They'd buried Samuel beside her mother's grave in a quiet ceremony yesterday, and with him she'd buried a part of her heart. Even knowing she'd see him again in heaven did little to ease the ache in her heart.

"How could Samuel have done something so foolish? He'd just written me with plans to go ice skating together this Christmas, and he was going to introduce me to Mattie." Leaning against the counter, Rebecca folded her arms across her chest and tried to blink back the tears. "Instead I met her at his funeral."

"She's such a sweet girl." Michaela wiped her flour-dusted hands on her apron. "I hope you get a chance to spend some time with her while you're home. This has been rough on her, as well."

Throughout the train ride to Cranton and during the following nights in her room, Rebecca had searched the Bible for scriptures that spoke of God as her strength and of clinging to her faith no matter what was happening around her. *Let us hold fast the profession of our faith without wavering (for he is faithful that promised) . . . Be ye steadfast, unmovable . . . Blessed is the man that endureth . . . Be strong in the Lord, and in the power of His might. . . .*

She'd played them over and over in her mind, longing to find that measure of peace that comes only from Christ. *I'm trying, Lord, but there is still so much I don't understand.*

Luke had asked her many of the same

questions she was asking now. He wanted to know why God had allowed the *Liberty* to go down, saving some and letting others die. She wanted to know the same things concerning her brother.

"Why does God allow things like this to happen? Samuel was taken while a killer lives." Rebecca's hands balled into fists at her sides. "How can murder be part of His will?"

"Sin is never part of God's perfect will." Michaela built the pie dough up around the rim of the pan then began pleating the edge into scallops, her face tense with emotion. "I'll never forget the night I lost Ethen and Leah. For weeks I couldn't believe they were gone. I can't begin to tell you how many times I asked God that very same question. It was one of the hardest things I ever lived through.

"But the Bible says that death's sting has been defeated by the amazing love of Jesus, who conquered it through His own death on the cross. I finally came to realize they were resting in the everlasting arms of our merciful Savior, something far better than life here on earth could ever be."

Rebecca retraced her steps across the kitchen to finish kneading the bread dough. "Knowing Samuel's in heaven doesn't take away the emptiness of not having him here with us . . . or the questions."

Michaela stopped pouring the prepared Marlborough pudding into the piecrust and turned to Rebecca. "What questions?"

"Questions of God's will for our lives. When I heard that Luke's ship went down at sea, I knew I'd lost him, but for some reason God saved him." Pounding her fist into the elastic dough one last time, she set it into a bowl then placed a cloth over it. "Why did God choose to save Luke but not Samuel?"

"I don't think that's a question anyone can answer," Michaela said. "The truth is, death is not something any of us can avoid. What we have to remember is that God has already conquered death, and we don't have to fear it. For the believer it's just a pause until we see each other again."

Rebecca placed her hands on her heart. "But it still hurts."

"I know." Michaela bridged the short distance between them and gathered Rebecca into her arms. "I'm so sorry you're having to go through this."

After a moment Michaela pulled back but kept her hands on Rebecca's shoulders. "It took a long time before I could freely let go of Ethen and Leah. Finally I realized the truth that they now sit enwrapped in peace and happiness at the feet of Jesus instead of in our temporary world of pain and struggles. They've seen the glory of God. And so has Samuel."

"It is an incredible thought, isn't it?" Rebecca wiped away her tears with the back of her hand. "I want to follow in His will, but even though I know heaven is a reality, it is still hard to imagine."

"That's because God's plans are always higher than our own. And it's only in following Him with all our heart that we can learn to discern what His will for our lives is."

"But how can I know for sure?" Rebecca gnawed on her lip, trying to formulate what she wanted to ask. "Like with Luke, for instance. I thought everything was so clear, but Samuel's death has brought up questions concerning my relationship with Luke. At times I'm just not sure what God wants from me."

"You knew you had to end things with Jake, didn't you? Maybe not as soon as you would have liked to have known, but I have no doubt God was the one who stepped in and intervened in your life."

"I'm not sure Jake would agree with that." Despite the somber subject, Rebecca let out a soft laugh.

"I spoke with his father not too long ago. Jake's doing well. He's living in Oregon, where he's a foreman of a ranch. And he's met someone. . . ."

"It's all right. I'm glad. I want the best for him."

"And God wants the best for you, Rebecca. If Luke is the one, you'll know. Trust Him."

Luke forced himself to make the final two strokes through the water then pulled himself out of the pool.

Peter Watkins threw Luke a towel. "She must be some girl."

"What do you mean?" Water dripped from his hair as he mopped the droplets off his face and regarded his friend out of the corner of his eye.

"You beat your record from last week."

"It's not enough, though. My upper body might be gaining strength, but the rest of me has a long way to go."

"Don't worry — it'll happen. Come on."

Luke frowned. "Haven't you pushed me enough today?"

"Remember, champ — today you're taking your first step."

Peter helped him to a pair of wooden

parallel bars then waited beside him as Luke struggled to find his balance. Standing there, his arms supporting his weight, he tried to remind himself why he'd been pushing himself so hard the past two and a half weeks. He could still see Rebecca clearly when he closed his eyes, and at night she floated through his dreams. The tilt of her mouth when she smiled, the soft cadence of her laugh . . .

But he had seen the look of hesitation in Rebecca's eyes as she'd kissed him that final time before leaving on the train for Cranton. So far she'd sent him two letters full of news about what was happening in the small town and with her family, but she'd written little regarding her feelings for him. It wasn't as if he doubted her love. No, it was something else. Something he'd seen in her expression that he couldn't put a name to or understand. Though he longed for her to confide in him, he had the feeling it was a personal matter she had to work out on her own. All he could do at this point was wait — and pray.

He'd promised her he'd be here for her when she returned, but he wanted to do more than that. As soon as he got his strength back and was able to walk, he was leaving for Cranton to be with her. The thought was like a bolt of energy shooting through him, and he willed his mind to focus on the task at hand.

Slowly he worked to ease the weight of his body evenly onto both of his legs.

"One step at a time, Luke. That's all you have to think about."

It was as if Rebecca herself had spoken the words. Ignoring the dull ache that spread through the limb, he focused on the mechanics of moving his leg. He set it down in front of him, and as he gritted his teeth from the pressure of his weight, Luke took his first step.

FIFTEEN

Rebecca played the mellow chords from one of Mozart's pieces then stopped as the ivory keys began to blur. Even music didn't bring her the joy it had when she first learned to play. But how could it when her heart was miles away from her parents' farmhouse? She missed Luke.

The last time she'd heard from him had been almost five weeks ago. He'd been struggling to gain his strength back. Now yet another week had passed without a letter. She ran the back of her thumb down the keys then pounded out a dissonant chord. A lone tear made its way down her cheek, and she wiped it away with the palm of her hand.

Trying to hold back the flow of tears, she pulled her lacy shawl closer around her shoulders and stepped outside. Winter had already begun to settle into the valley. The red, yellow, and orange leaves that had burst into color during the month of October had all but vanished from the woodlands. In their place were patches of white from last week's snowstorm.

She leaned against the wooden rail of the porch. In the distance Sarah and Anna hurried along the path toward the barn, swinging their metal buckets beside them. Their laughter, ringing through the cool evening air, brought a slight smile to Rebecca's lips. Familiar images like this helped to keep a degree of normality in her life. So much had changed since that night Aunt Clara told her Samuel had been killed. So many things she wished she could go back and change. But life didn't work that way.

She'd stayed in Cranton partly for her own need to be with her family, but also because of Adam. Her younger brother had witnessed the last seconds of Samuel's life and still struggled to let go of the guilt over the fact that he hadn't been able to stop the tragic event. Maybe he never would completely forget that fateful moment when Samuel's life was taken, but if she could help his heart and mind to mend, she'd stay as long as she was needed.

Drawing in a deep breath, she shivered under her light wrap. Before long the sun would drop below the horizon, leaving brilliant streaks of pink and gold behind. Then night would settle into the valley, wrapping a blanket of darkness across the rambling farmlands and forests. After Samuel's death nighttime had brought with it a myriad of doubts, reminders of her ongoing search for God's will and the occasional uncertainties about her relationship with Luke.

For the first time in months, though, her doubts toward God were beginning to dissipate. She'd taken Michaela's advice to heart. How could she follow God with all her heart if she didn't really know Him? His ways were higher than her own, and the more she tried to learn those ways, the hungrier she'd become to know His Word better and experience a deeper sense of His presence in her life.

The front door slammed shut, and Rebecca turned to see her father stroll across the porch toward her. Except for a slight graying around his temples, he'd aged little in the past few years. She was sure it was because of his marriage to Michaela. Love seemed to keep him young.

"I was enjoying your playing." He bent over and kissed the top of her head. "Up until the last chord, that is."

"Very funny."

Rebecca drew her arms around her father's waist and laid her head against his shoulder, wishing she were a little girl again. As a child nothing had really mattered, because her father had always been able to make everything right. It didn't seem quite so easy anymore. Spilled milk was much easier to mop up than a broken heart was to mend.

Her father rubbed the back of her head with his hand. "You miss him, don't you?"

"Samuel?"

"Actually, I was thinking about Luke." He wrapped his arm around her shoulder. "I know we all still miss Samuel. Always will for that matter."

"It still hurts." Rebecca frowned. "There's a hole in my heart that will never be filled."

"I know. I feel it, as well. Sometimes I wake up in the morning, and I've forgotten he's not here anymore. Then it all hits me that he's never coming back."

"At least I'm not blaming God for Samuel's death anymore."

Her gaze drifted across the snow-laden landscape to where the lacy boughs of the elm trees stood in all of winter's glory. The flowers had faded away with promises to return in the spring. God had created this world full of beauty and goodness. It was man who had corrupted it with evil.

"What about Luke? You haven't spoken of him lately."

Rebecca nudged her father with her elbow. "You're persistent, aren't you?"

He squeezed her shoulder. "When it comes to my children, I am."

She wished she knew how to put her feelings into words. She had no doubt that the stress of the past few weeks had altered her sensibility. "I haven't heard from him for weeks."

"There could be a number of explanations. Recovering from an accident isn't easy." He smiled. "Besides, I don't know a man alive who would win a blue ribbon for letter writing."

Her father's positive outlook did little to change her somber mood. She'd tried to justify Luke's lack of communication without avail; yet there had to be an explanation. "If nothing else, he could dictate a letter to his mother or send me a telegram."

"That's true, but I'd hate for you to make any snap judgments without knowing exactly what's going on." Her father turned her head toward him then looked into her eyes. "Because of my pride I almost lost your mother. Don't shut a door because of fear. Trust is a decision, Rebecca."

He was right, and she knew it. It just

seemed like forever since she'd told Luke good-bye. Sometimes she was certain he'd only been a dream. Her mind tried to make sense of the storm of emotions raging within her. Her feelings might be irrational, but that didn't keep the lingering doubts from intruding.

Rebecca shrugged. "Whatever happens, this has all been good for me in one sense."

"How is that?"

"I've decided to stop second-guessing God." She pressed her fingers against the edge of the rail. "In talking to Michaela I've realized that I've been looking for fulfillment in life through marriage and a family. I think what God truly wants is for us to seek Him with all our hearts, no matter what is happening around us."

Her father smiled again. "Those are pretty wise words coming from my eldest."

"I don't know how wise they are, but they do make sense. At least it's something I'm working on."

"And what about Boston? Are you planning to go back?"

"I think so." Gazing out across the white farmland, a part of her wondered how she could ever leave this place again. The other part longed for something more. "I was making a life for myself there. While I missed you terribly —"

"You'd better have."

Rebecca laughed, enjoying the light banter with her father. He was the one person in her life who always made her feel safe and secure. "As I was saying, while I did miss you, I really enjoyed working with Caroline. Plus, making the quilts for the children at the orphanage helped me feel as though I was finally doing something useful with my life. And then there's Luke . . ."

"So you've discovered God's will for your life?"

"I've discovered that serving Him is His will for my life."

She'd have to wait and see how Luke fit into that plan.

Luke stared out across the choppy gray water from the edge of the widow's walk, watching as each ripple followed its intended path to the shore. It was one component of life that never changed. The sea worked in one continuous rhythm, pressing wave after wave toward the shore. It was like the plan for summer to turn into autumn, and autumn into winter. It was all part of God's design.

If only life were that simple. But it wasn't. Luke had spent his entire life doing the predictable, but now he was finally ready to break away. Leaning against the wooden rail, he watched the white sails of a ship make its way toward the harbor. There would be no more voyages for him. No more rush of adrenaline as his whaling boat slid into the surf, prepared for the hunt. The only trip he had plans to make was one to Cranton — and Rebecca.

She'd been on his mind since the moment he had kissed her good-bye. He dreamed about their starting a life together — something that had been impossible before the accident. Only one obstacle hung between them. Her letters were full of colorful anecdotes of her family. The joy she felt being with them again was obvious. Once she decided to stay in Cranton for good, it would be only a matter of time before Boston would become nothing more than a faded memory.

It was something the two of them would have to discuss. While he had no longings to captain his own vessel, his desire to build ships had grown stronger. Dwight Nevin assured Luke that as soon as he recovered from the accident, he would have a job at the shipyard. What he ultimately dreamed of, though, was having his own shipbuilding company. Something he could never do in

Cranton.

He'd found a verse in Romans chapter twelve that had become pivotal in helping him answer the lingering questions. It was so significant that he'd committed it to memory. *"And be not conformed to this world: but be ye transformed by the renewing of your mind, that ye may prove what is that good, and acceptable, and perfect, will of God."* The verse was clear. In order to find out what God's will was in his life, it was necessary for him not only to be unconformed to this world, but also to be transformed by His Spirit.

For the past few weeks he'd done more than simply work to restore his physical condition. He'd taken the time to delve deeply into God's Word. He realized how he'd always done what was expected of him — and that God might have something else in mind for his life. It was time to trust fully in Christ for everything he needed. Even if that meant going against a long-standing family tradition. It was time to tell his mother how he felt.

Turning, he made his way slowly across the balcony and down the narrow stairs into the house. The muscles in his leg burned beneath him, but he refused to give in to the pain. The past few weeks had brought about remarkable progress. Three days ago he'd thrown away the wooden walking stick. Now he worked to make sure each step was steady so he didn't shuffle across the floor.

He found his mother in the kitchen, fussing over a simmering pot of soup. Bowls and pans lay strewn across the countertops. His mother's interest in cuisine was nothing new but remained a fact that amused Luke, considering she had a full-time cook and seldom ate what she prepared.

"Where have you been, Luke?" She glanced up, a marked look of frustration across her face. "Vincent Sawyer and his family will be here in less than thirty minutes for dinner. He's looking for some new men for his crew, and now that you're walking again —"

"Mother, I'm not going on another voyage." The words came out sooner than he intended, but he wasn't going to put off telling her his decision any longer.

"Of course you are." She waved the wooden spoon in the air, seemingly dismissing what he'd said. "Your leg is almost healed, and by springtime, when the *Marella* pulls out again, you'll be as good as new. This isn't an opportunity to pass up —"

"This has nothing to do with my leg. It has to do with what I plan to do with the rest of my life." He took a step forward so he could lean against the counter and take some of the weight off his leg. "Being a whaler isn't my dream."

The spoon clattered against the tile floor as she turned to him. "What are you saying?"

"I'm not going on another voyage." His jaw clenched with determination. "Not with Captain Sawyer . . . not with anyone."

Her face paled. "You're serious, aren't you?"

Instead of the bout of frustration he expected, a growing sense of peace settled over him. "I'm very serious."

His mother's shoulders slumped. "I always thought it was your dream. That's why I've encouraged you."

"It was your dream. Yours and Father's." Reaching deep inside, he worked to find the words that would help her understand that he needed to follow his own dreams. "The future isn't in whaling anymore, and —"

"I've heard all the arguments, Luke." Her face softened, and he detected the hint of a smile behind the wonder in her voice. "What I want to know is how much of this decision has to do with a certain young lady you've been pining over the past few weeks."

Luke shook his head. "I made this decision before the *Liberty* ever took sail. It was going to be my last voyage. It just ended a bit sooner than I expected."

"Why didn't you ever tell me this was how you felt?"

He'd expected her to put up a fight, but instead she sounded surprisingly relieved with his decision.

"You've always told me you wanted me to carry on the family tradition like my father and his father before him. Letting you down has never been easy for me."

"I've been told a time or two that I'm a hard woman to please." She took a step toward him and gathered his hands between hers, the grin across her face broadening. "I thought it was what you wanted, so I was determined to ignore my own fears. You can't imagine how much I dreaded your going off to sea each time. Losing your father was so horrid. I can't imagine losing you, as well."

The change in her countenance astonished him but brought a measure of relief at the same time. "Your life has always been so caught up in the sea and family tradition. I was afraid you'd regret my decision."

"All I've ever wanted was for you to be happy." She drew him into her arms for a moment then pulled back and caught his

216

gaze. "There's still one question you need to answer."

"What's that?"

"What are you still doing in Boston when the woman you love is in Cranton?"

Sixteen

Rebecca lifted the hem of her heavy wool dress and stormed into the barn, where her brother saddled up his black stallion. She hadn't meant to overhear the conversation between Adam and Jethro Wright, but their shouts had been loud enough for the neighbors to hear. Jethro's claims that he had a lead on Samuel's killer turned her stomach sour, considering she was convinced Jethro simply wanted to get his pudgy fingers on the reward money. He knew Adam well enough to realize her brother would jump at the chance to take revenge into his own hands, which is exactly what Adam had told Jethro. Adam planned to go after the man — alone.

She scurried into the darkened stall, stopping only to catch her breath. "Adam, I heard you and Jethro talking about going after Samuel's killer. You can't do this!"

"You can't stop me, Rebecca." He finished

cinching the girth beneath the horse's belly then turned to face her. "Have you forgotten this man killed our brother? No one else seems willing to do anything about it —"

"That's not true. There's a reward out for his capture, and Sheriff Briggs is following any leads he has." Desperate to stop him from doing something foolish, she gripped the sleeve of his leather coat. "He's a killer, Adam, and you're going to end up his next victim if you're not careful."

Jerking away from her clutch, he led the horse into the pale afternoon sunlight. Dark storm clouds were gathering in the east. If he went ahead with this ridiculous quest, the weather might prove just as dangerous. And there was no telling how long it would take to track the man down.

She followed him, not finished with what she had to say. "You're not thinking straight because you're too angry. Bounty hunters are already looking for him. We can increase the reward —"

"I'm going after him, Rebecca." His cheek twitched as he slid into the saddle, grasping a loaded rifle in his hands. "Tell Father I'll be back when the job is finished."

"Adam, please . . ." *Lord, I don't know what to say to convince him.*

Adam pulled back on the reins, and the

horse whinnied, ready to go. "I have to do this."

She felt a surge of anger rip through her as she watched Adam head south on the road toward town. How could he be dim-witted enough to go after a murderer by himself? Stomping the heel of her boot against the ground, she weighed her options. Her father had gone into town, and her stepmother had taken the girls to visit one of the neighbors. By the time either of them arrived home, Adam could be miles away.

She glanced at the barn, where the rest of the horses were corralled. She could hear one stamping in the stall, ready for such a task — and she had no time to waste. Running inside the barn, she saddled one of the horses. If she went after Adam herself, she might be able to overtake him and somehow convince him to leave the settling of scores to the bounty hunters.

Moments later she mounted the horse, thankful for the warmth of the wool coat she wore. The horse responded to her urgency and tore off down the winding road. She'd have to keep a steady pace to catch up with Adam.

Please, Lord, protect him from his foolishness. If anything would happen to him . . .

The thought sent a chill down her spine. She didn't know her brother anymore. Adam had always been quiet and reserved, but since Samuel's death all he'd thought about was revenge. Revenge, though, wouldn't solve anything, and in the process more lives might be taken — possibly Adam's. She couldn't bear the thought of losing another brother. The wound from Samuel's death was still too raw and painful, and she was determined not to live through something like that again if she could help it.

And nineteen years old was far too young to deal with the likes of an experienced gunman. They knew little about Samuel's murderer, except that he was an immigrant. This fact had given rise to a growing prejudice in Adam's life and had been further inflamed by men like Jethro who worked to pass on their racist beliefs that never did anything but cause trouble. She knew how deadly the consequences of unrestrained anger and prejudice could be, and the thought of what might happen if Adam carried through on his threats was sobering.

The wind whipped against her face as she followed Adam's tracks. Just past the Carter homestead, the tracks veered off the main road. She pulled on the reins and slowed the mare. The horse stamped beneath her, not content to stand still. If Adam were headed for the town of Hayes as she thought, cutting across the valley would take a good bit of time off the ride. It would also make him harder for her to track.

The squeaky wheel of a wagon ahead caught her attention. She glanced up the road and sighed with relief as her father's wagon headed toward her. Nudging the mare with her knees, Rebecca galloped up the road, desperate to lose as little time as possible.

She caught a glimpse of a dark-haired man sitting beside her father then pulled sharply on the reins. The stress of the day was causing her mind to play tricks on her. She'd imagined seeing Luke in the distance a dozen times, but this time . . .

"Rebecca?" Luke jumped out of the wagon and with a slight limp ran toward her.

She slid down from the horse, certain she was dreaming. It had been so long since she'd heard from him.

"I missed you so much." He lifted her off the ground and swung her around.

"I can't believe you're here." Tears of joy streamed down her face at seeing him again. "And you can walk."

Still holding her hands, he pulled them against his chest. "I wrote and told you. Didn't you get my letter?"

"No, but that doesn't matter anymore. I'm just glad you're here." A sharp wind whipped against her face. She hadn't forgotten the urgency to find her brother. "Something's happened, Luke."

"What is it?" His fingers pressed against her arm.

She grabbed the reins of her horse, addressing her father as his wagon stopped beside them. "Adam's left. He heard a rumor that Samuel's killer is working north of here. He's left to go after him."

A shadow crossed her father's face. "How long ago did he leave?"

"Ten minutes. Fifteen at the most."

"Where's he headed?"

"North toward Hayes, and he won't stop until he finds the man. You could go into town and get a posse together."

Her father adjusted the brim of his hat as he considered the choices. "Going back into town will lose valuable time."

Luke took a step forward. "I'll be happy to go with you."

"You can't go." Rebecca shook her head. "What about your leg? You're still limping, and it could be days before you return —"

"I'll be fine. I've faced worse situations before."

Don't go. Not just when I've got you back . . .

This time Rebecca didn't try to hold back the tears. The strain from the past few weeks, along with Adam's leaving and the emotional shock of seeing Luke, was more than she could handle. His notion to chase after Adam was as foolish as her brother's quest to bring in a murderer single-handedly. One of them would get himself killed.

"I just want to help." Luke's hand gripped her shoulder. "I'll be fine —"

"You can't make me a promise like that."

"Shh." He touched her mouth with his fingertips then wiped away her tears.

All she could do now was pray she didn't lose another man she loved.

Luke leaned back in the saddle, trying to stretch the weary muscles in his back. It had been almost thirty-six hours since they'd left the Johnson farm, and still they'd seen no sign of Adam. He and Rebecca's father had been able to follow Adam's tracks until last night, but now a fresh layer of snow covered the ground. All they could do was rely on what Rebecca had heard and hope they were continuing in the right direction.

He'd hated to leave Rebecca. The two months they'd been apart had seemed like an eternity, and then to see her so briefly before his unexpected departure to find Adam had been torture. At least he was sure of one thing. While he knew she was upset about his decision to go after Adam, he hadn't missed the obvious joy in her eyes when he'd arrived.

His ride on the train to Cranton had given him plenty of time to think. One thing had become clear. He wanted to marry Rebecca, even if that meant giving up his dreams of having his own shipbuilding business. There were always other opportunities. Boats ran along the Connecticut River, and surely there would be a need for someone with his skills. If not, he'd dreamed of raising horses as a boy. Maybe that was something he could learn to do.

With Rebecca's father beside him, he kept a steady pace, staying on the main road toward the town of Hayes. He knew it was important to join in the search, but a part of him wished he hadn't volunteered to come. His leg ached in the cold, reminding him he needed to take things slowly. He was thankful he'd been able to keep up so far, but he wasn't sure how much longer he could continue the rigorous pace.

A chickadee perched in a nearby tree, attempting to entertain them with his cheerful call. A flock of migrating birds beat their wings above them in the cloudless gray sky. He was amazed at how calm and peaceful the valley was. Except for the crunch of snow beneath the horses' hooves, it was surprisingly still — and beautiful. Snow glistened like tiny jewels in the morning sunlight. The landscape was a gentle combination of ridges and valleys, where meadows intermingled with thick woodlands, making a patchwork pattern like one of his mother's quilts. He could see why Rebecca loved this part of the state so much.

"Thanks for coming with me," Eric said, breaking the comfortable silence that had settled between them.

"I'm glad to be able to help, sir."

"How's the leg?"

Luke massaged the top of his thigh with his gloved hand. "It aches in the cold, but I'll make it. Compared to some of the situations I've found myself in at sea, I certainly can't complain."

Eric's rich laugh reminded Luke of Rebecca. "You'll have to tell me a story or two while you're here. I remember countless nights sitting around the fire, listening to my father-in-law speak of his adventures on the high seas."

Already Luke's memories seemed a lifetime ago. "I have a few of my own good tales to spin, I suppose. Stories of mutiny and legends of the monsters of the deep that at times rang true."

"Have you ever thought of writing your own chronicles?"

Luke chuckled at the thought. During his convalescence Rebecca's constant reading to him of adventures of heroes and heroines had been enough to discourage him from the idea. "I think I'll leave that to men like Herman Melville, who no doubt have a better grasp on weaving such tales."

A bough snapped beside Luke from the weight of the snow, reverberating like the muffled crack of a rifle. His horse started beneath him, and he pulled back gently on the reins to settle him. Scanning the horizon, he shivered in the wind, thankful for his wool coat, but selfishly longed for the roar of a warm fire. And for Rebecca.

"How many miles away do you figure the town of Hayes is?" Luke asked.

"I don't think we have much farther. Another mile or two at the most. We'll stop and talk to the sheriff to find out if he's seen

Adam or if he knows about the reward poster. If we can't find him there, I think we'll have no choice but to turn back."

"Unfortunately, I have to agree." Luke picked up his pace beside Rebecca's father, still feeling awkward at calling him by his first name as requested. "Finding Adam in this vast wilderness will be difficult without a clear idea of which direction he's gone."

"Samuel's death struck all of us hard," Eric said, his jaw taut. "Adam's never forgiven himself for not being able to stop it. In his mind bringing in the killer is the only way to absolve himself for what happened."

"Right or wrong, I think I'd feel the same way."

Luke remembered the overwhelming feelings of guilt he'd experienced over the loss of the *Liberty.* He still had moments when he relived the experience. Moments when he questioned God as to why he survived and others perished. He had no doubt Adam was struggling with many of the same questions. As he'd experienced in his own life, it was a difficult journey to go through. Until he'd stopped trying to fight God at every turn, he'd seen no relief in his future. Maybe God had brought him here for

228

reasons beyond his relationship with Rebecca.

Eric lowered the brim of his hat to block out the rising sun. "We've never talked about your intentions toward my daughter."

Luke wrapped the leather reins around his hand and slowed his pace. He'd been looking for an appropriate time to ask Rebecca's father for her hand. Now was as good a time as any. "I'd like to marry your daughter, sir."

"I had a feeling you'd say that."

Luke caught the slight grin on Eric's lips and breathed out a sigh of relief. The past day and a half spent alone with her father had been surprisingly amiable, but that hadn't erased Luke's feelings of concern, considering he was a virtual stranger to Rebecca's family and wanted her hand in marriage. "I realize you haven't known me long, but I love her and promise to take care of her."

Eric wrapped his scarf around his neck then stuffed the ends into the front of his coat. "My wife knew your mother back in Boston and speaks highly of her."

"I'm glad to hear that. My mother's a wonderful lady."

"Rebecca speaks favorably of you, as well, except for the fact that your letter writing leaves a bit to be desired."

Luke cringed. "Unfortunately, my mother has a habit of writing letters then forgetting to post them. I have a feeling she did the same thing with the letters I wrote while I was recovering; though, I confess, letter writing has never been my strong point."

"I'd say that's true for all of us men." Eric's laugh was quickly replaced by a look of concern. "Do you plan to take her back to Boston with you?"

Luke had expected the older man's question. He could only imagine how he'd feel when the day came for him to face the same thing with his own daughters. "I plan to leave that decision up to Rebecca, sir. Far as I'm concerned, as long as she says yes, I'll be happy wherever we live."

"Then I'll give you my blessing and hope Cranton wins out."

Luke smiled at his words as they topped another ridge and found the settlement of Hayes dotting the valley below them. Ten minutes later they rode into the sleepy town, dismounted, and tethered their horses a few yards down from the sheriff's office. The ache in Luke's leg was intensifying, but he worked to will the pain away. Stepping onto the boardwalk, he turned as two men flew out of the saloon and clattered onto the boardwalk beside him. The blond man landed a solid punch to his opponent's jaw before stepping into the street. The other man, his lip bleeding, staggered down the steps after him.

"Adam!"

At the sound of his father's voice, Adam hesitated, giving his blond adversary time to pull a gun out of his holster. Luke threw himself onto Adam, knocking him off his feet as the crack of gunfire split the morning air. The burning sensation of the bullet knocked the wind out of Luke as he slammed into the hard ground; then everything went black.

SEVENTEEN

Rebecca knelt on her hands and knees and worked in monotonous circles to finish scrubbing the living room floor. She focused on the straight grain pattern of the wood with its occasional knots, trying to control the fear she felt in the pit of her stomach. Four days had passed without news of Adam — or Luke and her father. She should have gone with them. At least then she wouldn't have been left to imagine what was happening. As much as she loved Luke, she was still furious he would risk his entire recovery to go after Adam. More than likely he was going to end up deathly ill from exposure to the cold because of his weakened condition.

Rebecca rubbed the floor harder, knowing she shouldn't worry about something she could do nothing about. It certainly wouldn't bring them back any sooner, and all it had accomplished so far was to give her a headache.

She glanced up as Michaela stepped into the room from the kitchen, her hands resting against her bulging stomach. Despite the tension she must have felt, an expression of peace crossed her face. "You're going to scrub away all the floor polish if you're not careful."

Rebecca wiped away the beads of moisture from her lip. "Sorry."

"Don't worry. I'm not complaining." Michaela smiled then skirted around the edges of where Rebecca worked. "Every time I turn around, you're a step ahead of me. I haven't had to do a thing to prepare for Thanksgiving dinner, and everything is ready for tomorrow. I really appreciate it."

"I've needed to keep busy." Rebecca leaned back on her heels and balanced her arms against her legs. "Do you think they'll be back in time?"

Michaela rested her hands against the wooden sill and stared out the window overlooking the front yard of the farmhouse. "If they're not here by tomorrow, then we'll wait and celebrate once they return. The girls will be disappointed. They're upstairs right now making decorations for the table."

Despite Michaela's optimistic front, the lines beneath her eyes were evidence she was also worried. Winter's fury had held off so far, but any day could bring signs of another storm.

With the back of her hand, Rebecca wiped the moisture off her forehead. "The pies and other dishes we made today will last only so long."

Michaela turned away from the window to face her.

"Is anything else bothering you?"

Rebecca let out a long sigh then began scrubbing again. "I'm frustrated at Luke for leaving when he has no business being out there in this weather. How could he risk his life when he doesn't have to?"

"He did it because he loves you, and Adam is your brother."

"I know." Rebecca stood and dumped the rag into the bucket, sloshing water down the sides. "But it seems foolish for him to risk his life to go after Adam when he's still recovering from his accident."

Michaela shook her head. "Luke's not Samuel, Rebecca. He's not out there because he's trying to prove something to you. Samuel made a bad decision and unfortunately paid for it with his life. I don't think that's what Luke's doing."

"I'm still scared." Rebecca gnawed on her bottom lip. "They've been gone so long."

"Love makes you vulnerable, and it even hurts sometimes; but when you find the right person, it's worth the risk." Michaela pushed back the edge of the red-checkered curtain and looked out the window. "And I'd say your prayers have been answered, Rebecca. Your father and Luke have just arrived with Adam."

"They're here?" Rebecca looked down at her stained dress and moaned, wishing she had time to change. "I'm an absolute mess."

Michaela smiled and reached out to take Rebecca by the hand. "You look fine."

Rebecca stepped onto the porch, a clatter of footsteps behind her. The girls must have been watching from their upstairs bedroom window, because Sarah, Ruby, and Anna ran ahead of Rebecca to welcome the men home.

She watched as her father got off his horse then reached down to toss Anna into the air. Even Adam looked glad to be home. For the first time in weeks, a smile covered his face. Rebecca's shoes crunched against the snow as she walked toward Luke. For the moment he was the only person she wanted to see. The scene faded around her until only she and Luke existed. All that mattered now was that he was here with her — and safe.

He slid off the horse, wincing as his boots struck the ground.

She reached out to grasp the edge of his sleeve. "What's wrong?"

"It's just a flesh wound —"

"What?"

The wind whipped against them as Luke pulled his coat back to reveal the bandaged shoulder. "I'm going to be fine."

Anger welled within her. "You should never have gone —"

"Luke saved my life, Rebecca." Adam stepped up beside her. "I found Samuel's murderer. Before he escaped he took a shot at me, and Luke pushed me out of the way."

"I'll be fine." Luke grasped her hand, his eyes pleading with her to believe him.

Blinking rapidly to stop the flow of tears, she watched as her father pulled Michaela into an embrace and nuzzled his face in her hair. The look of love in her father's eyes was unmistakable. Rebecca had always longed for a love like theirs. They faced life with God as the center of their relationship. And they trusted each other completely.

This was what she wanted in a relationship with Luke. He spent his life facing danger. It was a part of who he was and a reality he had learned to cope with. But his risk taking wasn't based on pride or even revenge. Her parents had been right all along. If she wanted her relationship with Luke to blossom into what they had, she would have to trust him.

Rebecca finished scrubbing the last kitchen counter and listened to the happy chatter coming from the parlor. Thanksgiving dinner had been wonderful, but the biggest blessing was that they were all together. The girls had worked hard at setting the table with their homemade decorations, as well as helping her clean up after the meal so Michaela could rest. The one thing she'd had little opportunity to do, though, was speak to Luke. While his wound was healing, the trip had worn him out, and he'd spent the past twenty-four hours resting.

Adam strode into the kitchen and kissed Rebecca on the top of her head. "Dinner was fantastic, Sis."

"I'm glad you approve." She flicked her rag at him and chuckled, thankful for the subtle changes in his attitude since his arrival home. She wasn't sure what had happened to put the smile back on his face, but whatever the cause, she was grateful.

"And I have to tell you another thing." Adam leaned back against the counter and crossed his legs. "I really like Luke. Promise me you'll marry him."

"That's none of your business." Her brother reached for another piece of pumpkin pie, and she slapped the top of his hand. "How many have you had?"

"It's Thanksgiving. I'm not counting." He swiped a piece of the dessert. "So are you going to say yes?"

"He hasn't asked me to marry him."

"He will."

"How do you know?"

"If ever I've seen a man in love, it's Luke." He popped a bite of pie into his mouth and grinned. "Remember — I spent a lot of time with him the past couple of days."

The reminder of that ill-fated quest sent a shiver down her spine. "You almost got him killed."

"I know. And I'm sorry." All signs of teasing vanished as Adam leaned back against the counter again. "On the way home Luke said some things that made a lot of sense. He shared with me his feelings of guilt when the *Liberty* went down."

"You still feel guilty over Samuel's death?"

Adam shrugged his shoulder. "Maybe I always will — I don't know. But at least now I've decided to try to let go of the guilt. And let God in."

Rebecca fiddled with the towel between

her fingers. "The same way I'm realizing I need to let go of my fears and let God reign in my life."

She'd begun seeking God with all her heart but had still allowed a web of fear to cover her. God didn't want her to be a woman steeped in worry. He had called her to rely on Him.

Wrapping her arms around her brother's waist, she squeezed him tightly. "I'm proud of you. I know this has been hard for you."

"In case you hadn't noticed, there's someone waiting for you outside."

Rebecca peeked out the window at the snow-covered terrain, where Luke was harnessing the horses to the sleigh. "What's he doing?"

"What does it look like he's doing? I'd say he's taking you for a sleigh ride."

Luke's breath caught in his throat as Rebecca stepped out of the house. She'd put on a hooded brown cape that covered most of her head but didn't hide her bright smile. Delicate flakes of snow had begun to fall, draping the countryside in their grandeur. She stopped in front of him, her breath leaving short vapors in the frosty afternoon air.

"You look lovely." He smiled at her and wiped away the snowflake that had landed on her cheek before it melted.

"Thank you." She took his hand and allowed him to help her into the sleigh. "How's your shoulder?"

"Sore, but I'm on the mend." The soft feel of her gloved hand left his senses spinning.

Once Rebecca was settled on the narrow seat, he joined her then wrapped a thick quilt around her. It had been too long since he'd been this close to her. The scent of her perfume tantalized him, and he longed to feel the sweet touch of her lips against his.

The horses started out at a slow pace away from the farmhouse and down the winding road through the valley. A cloudless sky hovered above them, and he could hear the muffled plodding of horse hooves as the snow crunched beneath them. Their sleigh bells jingled through the stillness of the day, a *clang-y* melody never to be written down.

He glanced at her profile. "Are you still angry at me for going after your brother?"

She shook her head and smiled. "But you did scare me. I've been so mad at Samuel for making a foolish choice that cost him his life. Then when Adam ran off, I couldn't believe he was doing the same thing. Putting his life at risk unnecessarily. When I found out you'd been shot, it scared me. I was so afraid I'd lose someone else I love."

He wrapped the lines in front of him so the horses could continue their leisurely pace down the road without a driver; then he caressed the back of her hand with his thumb. "You know my motivation was never to take a risk. I've always wanted a brother, and with all the stories you've told me about your family, I feel like I know them. I want to be a part of that. I want to be a part of your life."

A tear trailed down her cheek, but her mouth curved into a wide smile. "For so long I was afraid of the risk of loving you. I've realized now, though, that I'm more afraid of the risk of losing you."

"That's why I came — because I love you." Luke cupped her face in his hands, wiping away her tears with his thumbs. "I promised I'd wait for you as long as it took. I just couldn't go any longer without seeing you." He leaned over and kissed her gently, silent assurances of what was to come. "And there's one more thing."

"What is it?"

He reached into his pocket and pulled out a thin gold band, his heart beating with anticipation. "Rebecca Ann Johnson, will you do me the honor of becoming my wife?"

She nodded, wrapping her fingers around his hands and pulling them toward her heart. "I've found what I've always been looking for, Luke."

"What's that?"

"A man who could capture my heart completely."

The beauty of the snow-covered fields surrounded him. Towering pines reached to the heavens beside apple orchards and maple sugar farms. But at the moment he concentrated his attention on only one thing. The woman he loved.

"And your heart, Rebecca, is something I'll never let go of."

Dear Reader,

From the windswept Boston seacoast to the lush Connecticut Valley, Massachusetts, in the late 1800s is a place of unparalleled beauty and rich history. Writing these stories about Michaela, Rebecca, and Adam was like taking a step back into history for me and one I thoroughly enjoyed. It also was a journey of self-discovery for my own life. As my characters struggled to face life's challenges of loss, forgiveness, and finding God's will, I found myself learning spiritual lessons alongside them. What a wonderful reminder that in the midst of life's conflicts, faith can be renewed and love worth keeping found.

My prayer for each of you is that you might discover the freedom of following God with all your heart and that you might lean on Him no matter what circumstances you are facing right now. He is faithful.

Stop by my Web site at www.lisaharris writes.com. I'd love to hear from you.

Blessings,
Lisa Harris

The steps of a good man are ordered by the LORD: and he delighteth in his way. Though he fall, he shall not be utterly cast down: for the LORD upholdeth him with this hand.

Psalm 37:23–24

ABOUT THE AUTHOR

Lisa Harris is a wife, mother, and author. She and her husband, Scott, along with their three children, live in northern South Africa as missionaries. After graduating from Harding University with degrees in Bible and Family and Consumer Sciences, Lisa spent several years living in Europe and West Africa with her husband as church-planting missionaries. They have traveled to more than twenty countries, including France, Kenya, Japan, and Zimbabwe. Lisa has had over fifty articles, short stories, and devotionals published as well as two novellas and one novel. You can contact her at http://www.lisaharriswrites.com/.

The employees of Thorndike Press hope you have enjoyed this Large Print book. All our Thorndike, Wheeler, and Kennebec Large Print titles are designed for easy reading, and all our books are made to last. Other Thorndike Press Large Print books are available at your library, through selected bookstores, or directly from us.

For information about titles, please call:
(800) 223-1244

or visit our Web site at:
http://gale.cengage.com/thorndike

To share your comments, please write:
Publisher
Thorndike Press
295 Kennedy Memorial Drive
Waterville, ME 04901